Critical Acc

T0246725

"In *Zebra Crossing: Flashes of Desire*, Bruce Meyer leads us into new, lush worlds — hopeful, beautiful, and sometimes terrifying. Weaving delicate threads of southern Ontario Gothic, he quietly draws aside the veil and instantly plunges us into Hell, both geographical and existential. We visit decaying houses and trailer parks, the flaming water gardens of Pat O'Brien's bar, and meet Circe on a Georgian Bay island. We're immersed in the enchanting, elegant mathematical calculations found in love; witness a tragic afternoon tea, an intoxicating last meal, family tangles and terrors. We cannot turn away from executions, or murder by car, pitchfork and shovel. Zebras stampede through what may be either our material world or the regrets of a poignant imagination. In this stunning new collection, Bruce Meyer reflects us back to ourselves: vulnerable, torn, broken, longing, hopeful, and struggling; but always deeply human."

— Lynn Hutchinson Lee,
author of *Origins of Desire in Orchid Fens* (Stelliform Press, 2025)
and *Nightshade* (Assembly Press, 2025)

"There is some certain whimsical mystery to be discovered in Bruce Meyer's *Zebra Crossing*. This is an intelligent and amusing work that never ceases to delight."

— David Menear,
author of *Swallows Playing Chicken*

"Bruce Meyer offers a solution to the uncontrollable complexity of time by presenting places where time does not exist, most notably the writings of oneself and others. In poems such as 'Museum of Reading Habits' and 'Paragraph' the idea of timelessness is presented with a distinct grace that is reflected in the title of the collection. A level of elegance is sustained as Meyer traverses his way through the most grueling topics while simultaneously creating an inviting environment for the reader to bask in their melancholy and celebrate the inevitable fall from grace we are all forced to face.

— *Grace of Falling Stars*
review by Abby Coutinho, *South Shore Review*

"Meyer's writing is refreshingly earnest and reflective of how so many people have been feeling for the past year. A particular line from his first story 'The Yellow Jack' speaks volumes about the quiet ache that's been sitting in our throats for the past year: 'He was a dot on a map one minute, and a place that no longer existed the next.' Life's fragility contributes to the instability of our reality, and Meyer convinces the readers that it might be worth it to embrace the unknown and accept our newfound normal.

The stories reveal an underlying facet of the human experience that transcends historical generations; an unprecedented motivation to transform our lowest moments into inspiration to reach the highest peaks of mortality, as sometimes our darkest moments define the most radiant types of pure hope. Reminiscent of John Keats' classic 'Ode to Melancholy,' Meyer's whimsical writing reminds us that the most joyous sentiments are steeped in the lingering memory of tragedy which fuels us to ponder the dismal moments so we may celebrate and indulge in life's treasures when they come to us. From an accustomed love rejuvenated by music or a decrepit island united by a tight-knit community, Meyer presents a warm essence that bestows the book with both a timely and timeless flare."

— *The Hours: Stories from a Pandemic*
review by Abby Coutinho, *South Shore Review*

"Portraits of Canadian Writers could be described as an admirable project, but what takes the collection to an exceptional level is Meyer's devotion to and passion for Canada's literary legacy. His impressions of and meetings with these portrait subjects are memorably joyous, quirky, respectful, and poignant by turns, with his ultimate goal being to bring well-deserved recognition to such a diverse group and all "the dreams they put into words.""

— *Portraits of Canadian Writers*, PQL, 2016 (National Bestseller),
review by Meg Nola, *Foreword Reviews*

"By the grace of almighty God, my first literary translation work has been published. This Bengali book features various poems of Poet Bruce Meyer, renowned Canadian academic and inaugural Poet laureate City of Barrie, Ontario.

I express my sincere gratitude to Professor Bruce for allowing me to translate his amazing poems as well as for writing an amazing foreword for the book.

Poet Bruce's poetry shines light on the realistic illustrations of Canada's nature, beautiful layouts and positivity from every source of life. I am always touched by his works. Poet Bruce appears in different roles through his poems ~ sometimes as protesting teenager, a nationalist, general worker at the railway station, an affectionate father, a grateful child with a memory of the mother's two active hands or a dreamy teenager. Through my work, I want to present Canadian literature in Bengali, my mother tongue. Whatever gap exists in this area can be mitigated, among others, through translation works so people of two cultures and countries can learn about each other through its literary works."

— Farzana Naz Shampa, from the Introduction to the
Bangla edition of Bruce Meyer's Poetry

"Dying is not merely the domain of the dead; it is a shared experience. What remains after someone has passed are the memories, that reflections of the past and those who have passed, and the challenges everyone faces in the wake of loss. *Down in the Ground* is a collection of short, flash fiction stories that examine the ways in which individuals deal with grief and loss, not as morbid reactions but as attempts to understand what they are experiencing. From the cradle to the grave, *Down in the Ground* is a study in the complex creativity we use to address grief and to challenge death so that life can triumph.

— *Down In the Ground*,
Guernica Editions, review in the *49th Shelf*

What is your definition of a successful piece of writing? Who decides that?

Do not confuse success with perception of completeness. Success is for someone else to decide. A writer should never pat themselves on the back and say, 'I'm a success,' because that sort of perception is always short-lived. I have watched hundreds of writers come and go through my career. They had their moments and then were forgotten. The American poet Jack Gilbert in his poem 'The Abnormal Is Not Courage' ends with the great line that courage is 'The normal excellence of long accomplishment.' A writer is only as good as his or her current work and bringing that work to life means pouring their soul into it. But it is not for the writer to say what is successful or not successful. The writer is only permitted to say 'that works' and if it doesn't, to use his or her skill to fix the problems. A successful piece of writing by someone else goes 'Ping!' and that is when all the parts come together and the memory of the piece doesn't leave my mind.

— Sachi Nag,
Interview in *The Artisinal Writer* of *Toast Soldiers*

Can you talk about the title *Toast Soldiers*? What inspired it?

Meyer: The title was inspired by brunch. What I haven't told anyone is that I had a set of 78 rpm recordings by the Canadian comic, who lived and worked in England in the 1930s, Stanley Maxted, and his gem was A.A. Milne's "The King's Breakfast," which he set to music. The Milne poem is about hierarchies, ranks. It should be played in every office in Canada. "The King asked the Queen / And the Queen asked the Dairymaid / Could I have a little bit of butter for my bread..." The cow eventually gets the message but answers "Many people nowadays prefer marmalade instead." The poem is the classic statement on administrivia. My point is that inspiration, even in its most profound sense, does not come from profound places or ideas. The challenge is for the writer to drill down into a fragment of the commonplace and make it into something more than anyone could have foreseen with the source. Isn't that what resides at the core of invention?

What was the most difficult story to complete in *Toast Soldiers?*

Part of me wants to say all of them. Stories are easy to begin but the real work resides in finishing them. The hardest one to complete was likely "Oglevie," because the character is so beaten by life and the art of boxing. That story was inspired by Tolstoy's remark that there are really only two stories (and I had the feeling he was thinking of Homer's *Odyssey* which is the underpinning story in "Oglevie"). A stranger leaves town. A stranger returns. I kept asking myself if justice in an unkind, hostile universe, would be possible, and if even an inkling of it is possible, what would that justice (or call it mercy if you wish) look like? With the other stories, I can see then end the moment I thought of the beginning, and I knew what I had to do to reach the finale. Not so with "Oglevie." In the end, I gave him a shred of the mercy he deserved. I had been inspired by the line from Richard Hugo's poem, "Degrees of Grey in Phillpsburg" where Hugo says the misery won't let up "until the town inside you dies." The question I was wrestling with was "how does one find life and redemption in that town inside the protagonist when it is apparent to all the town has died?" Endings are never a problem for me, though getting to them can be a test of my wits.

— Interview with Bruce Meyer,
by James M. Fisher, *The Miramichi Reader*

"Meyer's prose, surprising and clever, runs from whimsical: 'Cheese explains so much about the type of person who ought to be murdered,' to downright unsettling: 'The noises in the forest had bodies and a body is always hungry.' Each story operates from its own world, in which the rules of morality tumble and shift in delightful mystery. The recurring theme of the absurdity inherently found within war is reminiscent of Vonnegut — there can be no higher compliment — but there is no mistaking Meyer's prose for anything but his own."

— Evelyn Maguire, *South Shore Review*

Zebra Crossing

Zebra Crossing

Flashes of Desire

Bruce Meyer

Library and Archives Canada Cataloguing in Publication

Title: Zebra crossing : flashes of desire / Bruce Meyer.

Other titles: Zebra crossing (Compilation)

Names: Meyer, Bruce, 1957- author.

Identifiers: Canadiana (print) 2024034541X
Canadiana (ebook) 20240345428

ISBN 9781771618205 (softcover) ISBN 9781771618212 (PDF)
ISBN 9781771618229 (EPUB) ISBN 9781771618236 (Kindle)

Subjects: LCGFT: Short stories. | LCGFT: Flash fiction.

Classification: LCC PS8576.E93 Z17 2024 | DDC C813/.54—dc23

Published by Mosaic Press, Oakville, Ontario, Canada, 2024.

MOSAIC PRESS, Publishers
www.Mosaic-Press.com
Copyright © Bruce Meyer 2024
Cover Design: Amy Land

Printed and bound in Canada.

 ONTARIO ARTS COUNCIL
CONSEIL DES ARTS DE L'ONTARIO
an Ontario government agency
un organisme du gouvernement de l'Ontario

Funded by the Government of Canada
Financé par le gouvernement du Canada

 Canadä

 ONTARIO CREATES

MOSAIC PRESS
1252 Speers Road, Units 1 & 2, Oakville, Ontario, L6L 2X4
(905) 825-2130 • info@mosaic-press.com • www.mosaic-press.com

That had to be the answer. When you heard hoofbeats, you didn't think zebras.

— Stephen King

"I refuse to prove that I exist," says God, "for proof denies faith, and without faith I am nothing."

"But," says Man, "the Babel fish is a dead giveaway isn't it? It could not have evolved by chance. It proves you exist, and therefore, by your own arguments, you don't. QED."

"Oh dear," says God, "I hadn't thought of that," and promptly vanishes in a puff of logic.

"Oh, that was easy," says Man, and for an encore goes on to prove that black is white and gets killed on the next zebra crossing.

— Douglas Adams

Contents

Torpedoes

Her mother and father lived in Hell. Parts of Hell could have been a form of punishment, but other areas were okay. The visits to Liz's folks were difficult.

Liz grew up in a cluster of houses built in the Thirties with green lawns flowing to the street. Getting there was hell. We'd cross the border from the safe, pastoral quiet of Windsor by the Ambassador Bridge and drive through Detroit. Liz grew up in Hell, Michigan. I would have said it was no hell. It failed to charm me the first time I saw it.

"I had a happy childhood in Hell," Liz always insisted.

The road to Hell was being paved every year. Signs hung from the lampposts on Michigan Avenue.

"Don't get out of your car."

What the signs meant was don't even think of slowing down or lowering a window to ask directions. People in that part of Detroit could smell weakness. They are sharks.

I walked in on a robbery in progress at a gas station. The bulletproof glass cubicle where the cashier sat was wide open. One man had a shotgun to the head of the cashier and another, standing lookout, leaned on the doorframe and tapped the business end of his sawed-off in his left palm. He was, how shall I say it, calm and polite.

"If I were you, I'd get in my car and gas up somewhere else."

I thanked him for his kindness, but I turned and asked, "How do I get to Hell?"

"Look around, Bud. You're standing in it."

After circling the downtown several times, and driving past King's Bookstore twice, I pointed out Tiger Stadium to my son and said they had good red hots there although the team was no hell. They did have a pitcher who was showing promise, a guy named Denny McLain who eventually won thirty games in a season, but fire and brimstone couldn't help the Tigers out of the basement.

"It must be hell to be in last place for so long."

Liz pleaded. She wanted to get out of Detroit and go straight to Hell. I didn't mind the experience, nor did my son who saw a different side of life and possibly death. We slowed at the robbery station. The hold-up men had departed. They must have filled up for free. A nozzle lay on the ground. The attendant was gone.

"I want to go to Hell," Liz said.

We found our way out of the labyrinth.

I had a dream once when I ran a fever. I was asked about the after-life. The answer has stayed with me. Hell is a question, an equation that can't be solved. Purgatory is how the question is solved, and the answer is Heaven. Dante could have saved himself a lot of time had he realized that.

Liz's mother, Helen, met us as we pulled into the driveway.

"I should have told you about the detour. Eventually, you'll be able to get to Hell sooner, but for now, the area around the Ambassador Bridge is a bit tricky."

Liz's father Hal was watching the television. He'd spotted a stain on his trousers that likely happened during lunch and without looking up he kept scratching at the spot on his elastic waist khakis, and said, "You made it."

"Were you expecting we wouldn't," I asked?

He simply laughed, though it wasn't a chuckle or a belly laugh but more a breathy huh? Hal could take all the fun out of fun. I sat and watched the television. It was overbearing. It was a court. The host was more interested in hah-hahs than jurisprudence. I couldn't help but feel glad not to be a plaintiff. Noise. People jumping up and down with pitiful glee. The court was out of order but it was part of the hell of daytime television.

Dinner was equally silent until Robbie asked Hal about the war. I had told Robbie repeatedly not to raise the subject with his grandfather. Hal had a terrible time, Liz told me.

"What was World War Two like for you, Grampa?" Hal's hands began to shake. He set down his cutlery and wiped his mouth on a napkin. There was a long silence. I told my son to eat his green beans.

2

Hal turned to me and shouted, "Leave the goddamned boy alone. Can't you see he's curious and wants to know? If I don't answer his question the story will die with me and my shipmates."

There was a long silence. I wanted to ask for gravy or for someone to pass me the pepper but both were right in front of me.

"Well, son, I served on the U.S.S. Indianapolis. Ever heard the story? We delivered some secret cargo to an island south of Japan. Our mission was top secret. We didn't know where we were. The Navy kept our whereabouts top secret and the person who knew where we were took R&R during our voyage back. He probably figured our mission was accomplished. We were also under radio silence."

"I was sitting in my anti-aircraft bay, having checked and cleaned my guns when I looked overboard and there were these straight white lines as if someone had drawn chalk marks on the ocean. I shouted, 'Fish! Fish!' and everyone thought I'd seen flying fish, fish that leap so high out of the water they look as if they have wings. I should have shouted, 'Torpedoes to starboard.'"

"A Japanese sub caught up with us and put two fish – our term for torpedoes – into our side even though we had Asdic and radar and extra plating. It was such a fine, sweltering July day, the operators probably knocked off to have a smoke.

I sat there and watched. There was nothing I could do. I knew what was about to happen. People see traffic accidents in slow motion. I felt paralyzed and kept shouting, "Fish! Fish!," but no one understood what I meant. I should have shouted ice cream. That would have gotten someone's attention.

Then, just forward of my gun bay, there was an explosion followed by a second blast down the hull. The Indianapolis shook as if it was that pepper shaker in front of your Dad he keeps staring at because he's looking for a way to change the topic,"

"I've never told anyone what happened next. We began to list to starboard and our bow began to sink, and even though general quarters had been sounded, most of the guys were below decks playing cards, eating in the mess, or taking forty winks in their bunks. The announcement came from the bridge: abandon ship.

I didn't know what to do, so I lit a cigarette until we began to roll over like an old dog. I could see the bridge and the stack pointing to the horizon and decided I'd better get in the water and be free of the ship because when a ship sinks, the suction pulls everything down with it.

Oil was burning. I swore I could see a third fish aimed at our midship. I tossed my butt in the gun bay and leapt for my life. Then I swam like hell. I turned and heard screams coming from the midship where the third torpedo hit. Men who'd lost an arm or a leg were begging for help as the Indianapolis slid beneath the waves."

"For the next four hours I swam as far away as possible until, exhausted, I lay on my back with my arms and legs spread. I floated. The last thing I remember was staring at the sun until I was almost blind and thinking, 'This is how a sailor dies at sea. I said God I'm all yours. Send me to Heaven or send me to Hell. I've made my peace. I die knowing I loved and was loved.

I was certain I heard my late mother saying, 'Not now, dear.'"

"Out of nowhere, a raft bumped into my head. In it were three guys, mangled, burned, all dead. I hauled myself into the inflatable – that's what we called them – and tossed the three bodies into the ocean, saying a prayer for each as they sank in the depths. When they were in the water, their arms raised as if they wanted to hold onto life. Each had a look of astonishment on his face. I can't forget that."

"I don't know how long I floated. I was thirsty. I kept thinking about what I'd give for a cold beer. There was a bar down the street from my home and I loved to go there on summer afternoons because the place had air conditioning. Cool air and a cold beer were all I wanted. Schlitz. At that point, any brand, freshly pulled from the bartender's pump, would have been a gift from heaven."

"I was half asleep when a voice called from the water. He begged to join me in the raft. I said 'Sure. I could use the company.' He'd been floating on a plank for three days and as he handed it to me as he climbed in he got a sudden look on his face that wasn't shock or surprise but exclamation as if something startled and surprised him. Then he was pulled back into the water. After the Indianapolis sank, the survivors were picked off one by one by sharks. I never saw him again as he disappeared in the depths but an arm floated to the surface. I spent hours clubbing those damned fish as I fought for my life."

Robbie spoke up. "What happened next, Grandpa?"

Hal fell silent and stared at the food. "See what's on TV, Helen. I'm finished here." My mother-in-law took my grandson into the kitchen with the promise of milk and Toll House cookies. I sat there not knowing what to say. Under the circumstances, nothing may have been the best thing I could say.

That evening when I thought everything had settled down, I asked Hal what brought him to Hell. I knew the story but I wanted my son to hear it.

"Your grandmother," he said ."I fell in love with her. I used to make jokes when we were first married about her cooking coming from Hell's Kitchen because she burned everything. I've spent the better part of my life in Hell. My happy Hell. Hell is the stories we keep."

I was awakened in the night by the sound of someone shouting. "Fish! Fish!"

It was Hal. My wife said he had nights like that since the war.

"In his mind, when he had his terrors, he was back on the Indianapolis and trying to warn his shipmates about the torpedoes. The hard part for him was the futility, that moment when he knew the inevitable was going to happen and could do nothing about it. Old friends said the war changed him. He understood helplessness. Hell is about being helpless."

I lay in the dark and thought about the endless horizon of the Pacific, the loneliness he must have felt, and the luck that he, of all people, was carried away from the cluster of survivors and picked up by a Catalina flying boat. When he got back to Hawaii, an officer told him he had his nerve breaking off from the main pod of survivors.

"Are you aware that while we were saving you we could have saved ten others? What makes you so special?"

Luck is what leads one to Hell. Hal once asked Helen why he was so lucky. His life in Hell was happy and nondescript though he couldn't abide the sight of blood, fire, or the ocean. He tried to go lake fishing once but broke down because he was terrified he'd catch an arm or raise the souls of the dead he tossed overboard.

Argus

I ask the dog what he thinks. He is an old dog and he lies beside my desk and farts when I try to work. I know wherever I go he will follow me. He is a good companion.

I stare out the window. Late autumn rain falls on the garden and the boughs of the trees cry because they have nothing to do but wait months while they are dead to the world. When they drop their leaves and their sap stands still in their branches, they are no longer trees in my garden but forests in a place that doesn't exist. Every year they die in the same way. They must understand how it feels to die and then return from oblivion. Oblivion is the difficulty all things face but few survive to describe it.

My wife senses my restlessness. She looks up from her book and asks if I couldn't find something to fill my time. I smile and tell her I spent the night in oblivion. The truth is I hate sleep. The past beats up on me. The dead insist I pay attention to them. I used to love sleep. Before I married, I had a small flat not far from the market, and to make my space complete my mother bought me a reclining chair. I would wake from delicious repose. Even frenetic music, a Shostakovich symphony, for example, could put me out cold.

One afternoon my power to dream ceased. How could I be certain I had not sunk deeper into vast darkness inside my head? Nothing appeared to make sense. I was on a small, wooden ship and the sea was blue and sparkling before the sky clouded and the ocean became wine-colored. The dreams troubled me. I was struggling to get home but I couldn't remember a note of Shostakovich, not even the haunting second movement of his Second Piano Concerto written on a February night or the final bars that conclude with a clock chiming five a.m.

I could not recall owning a reclining chair, or even my wife's face though I was certain I had a wife and she was calling me home. My friends had drowned – they hadn't written books or hung out in coffee bars with me to discuss Tolstoy or Dostoevsky. I even recall the taste of coffee.

Piece by piece, my life, memories, and things I loved evaporated the moment I remembered them. I closed my eyes and sawdust, death, blood, and men screaming on a plain before a walled city. One of the towers had thin white curtains that danced in the breeze and a woman on the battlements shouting the names of those who were about to die.

One of the worst pains one can feel comes from knowing there is one person I loved more than others and she was fading into a shadow – her smile, her green eyes, the touch of her hand in the night when I almost woke – and the whisper of snow falling against the walls of the house. And then, I forgot the sound snow makes when it is driven by the window, and I felt its absence the way the loss of feeling in a finger asks one to recall something that cannot be remembered or touched. Oblivion is the confusion of one narrative with another, the layering of realities as if in a delusional state, and only my own story mattered to me.

I was ready to toss myself overboard and drown when I remembered an old man puffing on a cigar. He had a close-cropped white beard and panes of glass sitting on his nose, and he turned to me as an aside from arranging strange little statues on a shelf behind his desk and muttered how I was living the story of a man attempting to wake from a dream.

The sea before me was endless but an island, slanted in the opposite direction from all the others loomed out of the mist one morning and I knew I had arrived. I clambered up the cliff face. An old dog walked up to me and I bent down to rub him behind the ears and he sat on his haunches and licked my hand as he looked at me as if I had just returned home without explaining where I had been and why I had been gone so long.

Table H

I work as a server for afternoon tea at the King George Hotel. The hotel is old so you will have to gather for yourself which King George has the honor of being the hotel's eponym. My domain is composed of tables H, I, J, K, L, and M, bringing trays of *petit fours* from the kitchen, jugs of hot water from the enormous silver samovar in the corner of the dining room – the samovar is merely a front for a less than spectacular hot water pipe – and offering agreement with people's choices even when I know that the Lavender Darjeeling is not half as fine as the Starfruit Oolong, but what do they know? They're going to drink it, not me.

There was one couple who came in every Sunday afternoon precisely at two p.m. and sat at their reserved table, table H. To hear them one would think they are divorcing. They despise each other. They would rather spend time with anyone on earth than with the other. The woman, let's call her Marjorie, even propositioned me once while her husband, we'll call him Hubert, was in the gents. She said she had a room upstairs with a view.

I told her I had to work until ten p.m. when the last smoked salmon sandwich and macaron had been served. My daughter, Aizza, would be expecting me to help with her mathematics homework. I wanted her to become a doctor.

When he returned he would inevitably tuck the edge of the table cloth into his belt so as he rose to leave, I would have a towel draped over my left arm and be ready to assist him in the reclamation of his decorum if the cups, saucers, and teaware slid toward him. It is my job to make people feel dignified.

Hubert and Marjorie were unique in that they were locals. Both always insisted that the saucers match the cups. The saucers, one of the fading formalities of high tea, were mainly Crown Derby, Minton. or Coalport. If there was even a smidgen of crust on one of the sandwiches, the matter would be drawn to my attention and I would return with the offending finger to the kitchen where the tea cook – he is not a cook but an arranger of items that have been prepared the night before every tea, no matter what the day – would look at me and say, "Not Table H again?" I would nod. It was part of the ritual of Sunday afternoon high tea.

Most of the guests were tourists. They wanted to know what a British high tea was, in all its glory. The King was located not far from the American border. Those who would never travel overseas would be seated at tables K, L, and M. I tried to leave I and J vacant unless we had an overbooking because the language of animosity at Table H often put people off their illusions of grandeur.

I would explain to the Americans that tea when it is served properly, must not be served on the boil and must steep for at least the length of the Lord's Prayer and no longer than the service for Committal of the Dead at Sea from the *Book of Common Prayer* or it would become bitter. Most had never read it and asked where they could buy a copy. They, of course, would argue with me that they wanted their Lipton in a glass carafe with the bag on the side so they could dunk it up and down. And, as a good tea server, I would agree with them though it gave me remorse to do so. I do not believe in dunky-dunky. That is gauche. But they are guests and the guests are right even though there were times I wanted to shout at them and tell them they had no idea about how the rest of the world lives, and they could take their ideas and go home. But I didn't.

Table H, however, came with its own set of problems: the complications of love. The animosity they expressed for each other was endearing and respectful over a no-man's land of violets or irises or tea roses arranged neatly in a silver setting. H stands for many things, and you do not have to stretch your imagination to understand that I am referring to a place of eternal damnation though no matter how harsh the exchanges were, revealing the most profound secrets of their lives, secrets I cannot, for professional reasons of discretion and gentlemanly service reveal to you, they never raised their voices. Hubert and Marjorie were always smiling.

I was serving their finger sandwiches and had just brought the newly christened pots to their tables when Marjorie beckoned and whispered she had a secret she wanted to share with me and her beloved husband, and she reached into the vase, drew out the little pink sweetheart rose, a lovely button with exquisite fragrance, and slipped it into the empty buttonhole of my server's jacket.

I patted it with my hand, thanked her, and told her I would wear it as a badge of honour for their generous patronage every Sunday afternoon at two p.m. when the rose slipped out and fell to the floor. Hubert stood up, oblivious to the fact that he was wearing the edge of the tablecloth in his belt buckle, and retrieved the flower from my feet as I, too, bent down. My thought was he was going to punch me, perhaps in the face. I did not relish an injury to my teeth or nose. Instead, without moving closer, which would have brought the service to the floor, he undid my name tag and pinned the flower to it before redoing the clasp. He patted it and told me I was a good man. He sat down and resumed the smiling *entente cordiale* with his wife.

The couple at Table H always ordered chestnut macarons and lemon *petit fours* with the cream icing between wafer-thin layers of chiffon cake covered with a yellow fondant with a hint of citrus and a candied sliver of lemon rind on top. But when they gave me the rose, I thought it best to speak their language of diplomacy which was the language of afternoon tea.

One is apt to confuse the unique natures of the partners in a couple, especially when the unspoken differences are so undetectable. This is not a problem one encounters on most days or at most tables. People bring in their aunts or grandmothers. The women are delighted and coo over the service. Their sons and daughters or nieces and nephews praise the ritual of afternoon tea and tip accordingly. It is all part of the art of being a good server. But Table H on Sunday afternoons was different. The maître'd knew not to sit anyone else at 'their' table. I think he, among all the staff, came closest to understanding what I came to learn about Hubert and Marjorie. He would often pass me if he overheard a snippet of conversation and roll his eyes as if to say, 'I don't know how you stand it,' but I would smile and shrug because I knew what each one of them wanted. It occurred to me that they were trying to find themselves, that after so many decades together, faithful decades as far as I could ascertain, I learned from their barrages they had lost themselves in the struggles of love. They were warriors of devotion.

Not only was I certain that Hubert was a Crown Derby Mikado man who imagined himself drawn in the bold deep sea blue strokes of a shogun, or that Marjorie pictured herself as the image of an Indian Tree with its solid green roots running into the base of the pattern, but that each saw themselves reflected in each cup they sipped. Neither took cream or lemon. They were stoically Earl Grey, straight up, and chose the blend with the richest bergamot nose. That was the one thing they could agree on. Traditional. Solid. No cream. No lemon. No sugar. The straight goods. The honest way to drink tea. They never watered the stock. And as they drained each cup down to the tea leaves, I knew they could see their own likeness in the meniscus of the green-brown liquid. The tint gave their faces depth. As they drank, each looked into their cup as if they were trying to find out what they looked like after a long life together.

They had been married, I learned one afternoon, for forty years, and that day, that precise moment I set their pots before them, was the exact moment of their anniversary. I congratulated them and told them time cherishes those things that are beautiful and lasting and enriches them with an elegance that life makes precious and lasting.

I may have gone too far.

The couple looked at me with surprise and burst out laughing. It was the one time I saw them laugh together, perhaps not at me but with me because they saw that I could see they were at war with each other in the kindest possible way, presenting themselves as pearls, as the aggravating grain of sand in each other's shells that forms a jewel. That, to me, is a beautiful thing.

They not only sat at Table H, but they were in H, that place of strange meetings where two souls experience a mutual dependency and fear one will crawl out of the cauldron first and abandon the other. I once heard a story about the fiery place that described eternal torment as the product of need, that just when one soul appears to climb out of the fire and brimstone the other pulls him back not because they are jealous that one of them is about to escape but because they share their pain as a bond.

That is why my heart broke when Hubert arrived one Sunday afternoon by himself. I stood silently, almost reverently, beside Table H, my hands folded in front of me as if I were praying in a Protestant church with my head bowed. After four or five minutes, of what felt like a proverbial eternity, I understood what H must be like, that real pain is not the punishment or the wrath inflicted on a soul, but the ache when that soul finds himself or herself alone and abandoned. He looked up at me. I could tell from the tears in his eyes he could not read the menu.

"What is it she always orders for us? I forget. Maybe I've forgotten because I never listened. What does Marjorie usually get?"

I felt as if I had fallen on a spear and driven the point even more deeply into my chest when I bent over to him, discreetly, of course, and asked, "Will she be joining us today?"

Hubert closed the menu.

"The usual today. The usual."

He paused and I did not move. I knew he wanted to tell me what had happened, and my feet felt as if they had grown roots and sunk into the floor like the Indian Tree in Marjorie's cup.

"My wife, my dear wife, passed on Thursday. I buried her yesterday. For the sake of ritual, I decided to take tea today to remember her."

I bowed and nodded. I wanted to express my condolences but all I could do was bow in respect.

Nothing in my years of tea service prepared me for that.

After I had served Hubert his finger sandwiches and set the sweets tree before him, I produced a bread and butter plate with a single rose macaron.

And after he had paid the check and I was clearing the table with the busboy, I realized Hubert had left the rose sweet where I had set it down.

Famous Last Meals

"Can you imagine what fun it would have been to have a sushi bar on the Titanic?"

It was good to see her again. We hadn't gotten together for a good meal in years. I hadn't the heart to tell her the flower garden behind her flat was overgrown with weeds. Our dinner made me nostalgic for the old times. I had almost forgotten our wonderful Saturday evening dinners when we'd meet at a quiet restaurant with a good wine list and finish the meal with a glass of late-harvest Vidal then go back to her flat so first thing on Sunday mornings over omelets and coffee we could discuss a book we wanted to write. It was to be a chapter-by-chapter exploration of famous last meals.

One of our earliest conclusions was that intentional last meals are horrible and it is a lucky thing for diners that chefs aren't mass murderers. Some, such as Ted Bundy, asked for steak and eggs, a truck driver's opening repast while John Wayne Gacy reinforced the idea of the scary kill clown. Gacy's last meal consisted of fried fast food. If he hadn't died by lethal injection, his diet would have done the executioner's work.

We skipped over the Last Supper. Bread and wine without fine charcuterie weren't appetizing to us. "They could have at least multiplied some fishes," she said, "perhaps some sashimi. Agonies in gardens are better on full stomachs."

What fascinated us more than Elvis' ham sandwich were the unintentional last meals, the elegant multi-course affairs served to the First Class on only the best liners. Those who tucked into their fare had no idea what awaited them, and when so much life was lost in a matter of hours, someone thought enough of the fare to save a menu from the dining room. For those fortunate First Class survivors, oysters and Consommé Olga must have seemed a distant memory as they shivered beneath the stars.

"Had they waited long enough, with foreknowledge of their fate, they could have had all the sashimi they wanted for free."

We debated the pros and cons of each menu. The Andrea Doria was a nice ship, but the menu was bland – as if someone had torn a page out of *Good Housekeeping* magazine circa 1955 about what to feed a hungry hubby after a long day.

"A wedge of a head of lettuce, chilled of course, with Thousand Island dressing? What were they thinking? Who would serve them that," she asked. The chef likely realized he had a captive audience and no one, no matter how desperate, dared jump overboard and swim to shore for something better. It was probably all to the good that ship capsize."

"How about the Lusitania," I said. "Yes, it was wartime, but the food mustn't have been half bad on the Cunard Line."

"That's not fair. There was a war on so the meals on the Lusitania weren't all that special because of rationing and the ship sank just after the first lunch sitting so the second sitting never had a chance to pick the larder clean. Besides, lunches tended to be less elaborate. The Titanic was an awful way to go, with all that cold water and ice, though one of the survivors was the bread and pastry chef who managed to pickle himself in cordial before leaping into the North Atlantic. The guy's name was Joughin, and he spent three hours in the freezing North Atlantic with little to no adverse effects. He was also likely eating the dining room fare which, to my mind, was the best among all the ships."

"So, you're going with the Titanic? Is that your final answer? Have you considered the Empress of Ireland? The first class was undersubscribed so the portions were slightly larger though they only got one meal in during the voyage before she sank in the St. Lawrence River," I noted.

"How about Charles I on the day of his execution?"

"I'm ahead of you. He had three coddled eggs though with his layers of shirts so he wouldn't appear to be shivering from fear or cold, he must have considered whether such a meal would stay down."

I felt her absence as I remembered those conversations. We'd drop by a late-night Tesco near Victoria Station and stock up for our experiment the following morning. If there were special ingredients, she would message a list to me and I would go into Fortnum's on my way home during the week and purchase the more exotic spices and a box of Rose and Violet Cream chocolates to seal the deal on a Saturday evening. She loved picking off the little pieces of candied rose petals and often remarked that if she had to have a last meal, it would be resplendent with flowers. In the garden behind her flat, we cultivated Johnny-Jump-Ups to garland a salad and pansies, in season, to add a peppery flavor to a soup.

The art of growing edible flowers didn't fade in the rich soil of her yard. Even after she accepted the transfer to Mississippi for a year, I tended the beds. I had grown accustomed to their colour and flavour in my meals. She was excited about the Mississippi job not because it was in Mississippi but because she found a flat in the French Quarter of New Orleans. She eagerly anticipated shrimp remoulade at Arnaud's and the buzz of the third Hurricane at Pat O'Brien's Bar amid the flaming water gardens that reminded me of hell.

New Orleans, alas, was where her problems began. Picture a public school-educated Oxford graduate who adored food but loved wine more arriving in a city that I described to her as the safety valve of middle America. On a Saturday night, for a three-block radius around Pat O'Brien's special level of Hell, we would stumble over men in navy blazers, cotton khakis, and button-wing blue shirt collars passed out on the sidewalk and surrounded by four or five boxes each containing a souvenir Hurricane glass.

The idea behind the tall, alcoholic drink was that one souvenir glass would make a person relaxed and happy. The second brought out exceptional, if absurd, creativity, and the third would make the drinker stagger or walk blocks on their knees. After that, the fourth or fifth Hurricane would send a person to a dark eternity on the far side of the moon.

The Hurricane was more than a liquid version of Huxley's soma. It was an invitation to self-destruction, the bottom of a follow-up meal that made one question why they paid for an expensive dinner. One evening we heard three people, presumably English professors, discussing who would play which position in the Norton Anthology of Major British Authors Baseball team. Was Coleridge a catcher? Should Chaucer be long relief if Shakespeare's arm got tired by the seventh inning? She didn't know much about the American game but by the time I finished explaining the language and plays and methods of scoring, she could have been a sports writer and joined the trio at the next table who, by that point, could hardly pronounce Auden.

I told her I had my heart set on the sea bass at Arnaud's. There was something the chef did with picayune spices that I wanted to try. I had also read about their Kaiser puffs, and how the exact temperature of the oil determined whether the squared slice of potato would puff according to plan. A plate of the Kaiser puffs was served with a Cajun mayonnaise that was far better than any dip I tasted in Belgium where they practice the same method of serving fries.

She stared at me as if I had lost my mind. "Don't let me stand between you and your food," she said and went off with the three professors who were now comparing poems to baseball because neither pays any attention to time. I sat at the restaurant table by myself. In true New Orleans fashion, a piece of bread that could have been made by Joughin on the Titanic was placed beside my water glass, no bread plate, because that is how one receives bread in the pelican city. It reminded me of the Last Supper as I sipped my wine.

Even the trial couldn't clarify what happened that night though the jury was quick to convict a foreigner. According to conflicting testimony, the man who could not pronounce Auden's first name had a friend who lived out on the Bayou. The friend has an airboat and for a hobby hunted gators in the dark by dangling a dead duck by the neck a few inches above the waterline. When the gator leaped up for the duck, someone in the airboat would shoot the predator. On their arrival at the Bayou house, there had been an argument about Donne and whether Donne was first base material.

The female professor or whatever she was had argued with my friend, insisting she knew nothing about baseball though my friend had studied all the great British authors – Yeats and Burns included as infielders and grabbed for the other woman's gun. The melee had been broken up but the insult had been noted. That's when my friend and the female professor went off in the airboat by themselves accompanied by a handgun, a pump-action shotgun, and a bottle of Jack Daniels. What happened next in the dark baffles me.

My friend said the woman didn't know how to use the shotgun and the recoil from a point-blank shot knocked the other woman backward into the Bayou. Dazed and confused and with her final appearance before the men, she panicked and tried to turn the airboat around, but in the dark, she lost her way. She might have been handed a reprimand for boating while intoxicated though almost everyone in New Orleans breaks that law. She might have explained the woman's death had her body remained submerged longer in the water where, even when they found her, the gators began their feast, consuming the wound to the woman's torso and the rosary that the coroner found in the belly of the beast – the men testified it belonged to their lost loved one – except that the gunshot wound wasn't consumed by a critter. The wound was from an automatic pistol and the bullet matched the gun the men had handed to my friend.

For as much time as my company would give me, I sat in a Louisiana courtroom as the droll prosecutor and the droll but inept defence attorney hemmed and hawed over the case. At times the judge appeared to lean his face on the balled fist of his left hand, and some of the jurors during the most crucial moments of testimony appeared to nod off. After all, what was an English woman doing on an airboat in the middle of the night in a remote portion of the Bayou? She didn't have to go gator hunting. She'd argued with the other woman. Her feathers had been ruffled. All the jurors needed was to add some tar to the mixture.

Murder happens far more frequently in New Orleans than I ever imagined. I sat one night on the bed of my hotel room and over the course of three prime-time hours, I witnessed fifteen murders, dramatized of course, for entertainment. I'm not used to that. I'd rather watch CNN or comedy dramas where country folk ride bicycles and the vicar saves the day for the local constabulary. Documentaries are slices of cake for my mind.

When she was asked what she wanted for her last meal, she was determined to make the system work for her in a way it hadn't functioned when she stood trial. I flew a red eye to New York and caught a shuttle flight to the south because she requested I be there with her. Perhaps she wanted to make one final statement to her captors or maybe it was the mischief in her that made us want to write a book about famous last meals, but she declined the Warden's offer of junk food or truck stop fare and demanded to be served the last meal from the Titanic.

Her order was, at first, met with disdain that made the news. English murderess wants Titanic menu. The issue made it to the floor of the state legislature where, after considerable debate, the lawmakers acquiesced to her wishes. A clause in the state's homicide code stipulated she was entitled to a last meal of her choice though the prison code wouldn't permit the serving of wine. Shortly before I boarded the plane, I received a letter from her in which she discussed the absence of spirits.

"No Last Supper for me. What a shame. Even Jesus, who they quote at every possible opportunity, got to have a drink to wash down his bread."

The prison where she was held was ghastly. Prisons are devoid of personality for a reason. For those on death row, they kill the spirit before the body can follow. She wasn't allowed to wear any makeup, and the nutraloaf, or disciplinary loaf, or whatever they called it day after day, precipitated a noticeable weight loss. She had described the odd meat substance to me, and after hearing her description I wanted to kill the person who had invented the rancid-tasting prison food.

The orange jumpsuit didn't do her any favors. I was strip-searched for contraband items before the bars opened to admit me.

We began our dinner with raw oysters and hors d'oeuvres accompanied by Consommé Olga with sturgeon marrow adrift like tiny lifeboats in a broth fit for a Czar. We opted for the poached salmon second course and Arnaud's embellished the serving with Hollandaise sauce accented with tarragon.

For the main course, she had the fillet mignon. To be different so we could sample each other's selection, I chose the Sautee Chicken Lyonnaise which is a way of saying someone made a classic cream sauce and spiked it with just a splash of Chardonnay and a hint of lavender.

"Is it chilly out tonight," she asked.

"Yes," I said as a waiter presented us with a cheese board, slices of fresh fruits that were mostly kiwis – something the Titanic chefs never served, and cups of steaming coffee to keep us awake and alert well past dawn. The stars were high above the prison yard, the night calm and windless, and Lake Pontchartrain was smooth as glass when a taxi drove me into the dawn and I checked my ticket and passport.

The Marriage of True Minds

Our two Gs, Gary and Gwendolyn, were what we called 'the perfect couple.' They thought alike, loved to discuss politics though they took opposing sides in a debate, and in terms of style he loved traditional things while she was what we called a 'life editor' who tossed out anything that seemed old. We sensed, however, that no matter how they mirrored each other's tastes, they were different in so many ways – she loved wine, he never drank...she loved fast cars, he cycled everywhere – we were certain their love had a higher purpose. We weren't sure what that purpose was but guessing about it kept us entertained.

We always hated it when members of our circle of friends split up, but it happens. In our circle, one of the things we loved was the fact that everyone was in a couple. It made for a nice gathering at a restaurant. The men could talk to the men and the women to each other, though sometimes we tossed that distinction aside and everyone contributed to a discussion. No one ever went too deep with a topic. It would not have been right. Couples keep things from getting too deep when they are with other couples.

When we got together we would gather at a local bistro or a Mediterranean restaurant – places that serve multiple things in small dishes we could all sample – and talk over dinner. The nice thing about couples is that no one ever takes the last of something. A dish of olives could make its way around the table and even if there was only one left we could pride ourselves that someone in one of the couples did the kind thing and left it for someone else and wouldn't complain about not getting anything.

Mezes are such a great idea. We would recommend the idea to other couples. Because people constantly pass dishes when they do mezses – Greek or Syrian food served in small dishes and in small portions where no one took too much – we could guarantee that both parties in a couple wouldn't be checking their cell phones and instead would be concentrating on putting just the right amount on their plate and passing the little dishes and raving about the taste of something and recommending the food to everyone else. Couples keep things engaged.

So after we left a Mediterranean place one night, the rest of us gathered discreetly down the block to talk about Gary and Gwendolyn and what was wrong with the evening. It was starting to rain, but we were concerned in a polite and not too deep way about why Gwendolyn kept checking her texts in the middle of the meal. She had driven to the restaurant. Gary had come on his bicycle. We questioned what passion made Gary peddle around in the rain, and why he kept passing and looking at us. We called to him as he rode by but he stared at us as if he'd never seen any of us before and kept peddling. He appeared to be looking for his wife's car parked on a side street. True minds create true mysteries, and there is nothing better for a group of friends to discuss than a true mystery.

The admitted impediment may have been our fault. Some of us already knew him from other circles of couples so we figured he'd be a safe bet, perhaps a social experiment, to interject him into our collection of couples. And it wasn't our idea. We invited the newcomer into our group at Gwendolyn's suggestion. She told us she worked with him which was her way of telling us that Gary had lost his job although we didn't ask him outright if he had. That wouldn't have seemed right. We won't name the newcomer who came by himself and who worked with Gwendolyn not because we didn't already know him. Most of us did. But because why should we? He wasn't part of a couple.

The newcomer and Gwendolyn shared a bowl of hummus, then, ordered the eggplant and the same wine. They didn't pass either the hummus or the eggplant. They talked about how good it was. We were aware Gary wanted some but the newcomer and Gwendolyn cut him out of the dishes and, with a note of sympathy to Gary, they cut us out as well. Gwendolyn and the newcomer were in their own little world, which is just wrong. Everyone was supposed to be part of a couple and the newcomer could have made things easier for us all if he'd brought someone along with him, even someone new, and we could have gotten to know her. But the point is he didn't. It was as if Gwendolyn and the newcomer were constructing a wall around themselves and it sort of spoiled the evening which is why we stood beside our cars on the side street and talked about it as if it were a catastrophe as the rain came down on us. Each of the couples had an umbrella and we gathered under them because that's what couples do.

We tried to interrupt Gwendolyn and the new guy by asking him questions to which we more or less knew the answers. We asked about things he liked to do for exercise, or where he'd spent his last vacation and he just stared at us as if what we wanted to know was none of his business. He and Gwendolyn talked incessantly about professional associates they had in common. Their connections were endless. It was annoying.

So when we got the news and the news spread among the couples about what had transpired we couldn't say we weren't surprised but just terribly sad. Gary and Gwendolyn had been a meeting of true minds. They weren't alike enough to be anything other than a couple. Their differences made them intriguing. They didn't need to speak to each other. They spoke to members of other couples who were also different as night and day from their partners, and that's what made them a great couple. They really didn't have much to say to each other but a lot to say to others.

So, only Gwendolyn understood why Gary peddled through the rain and why she ran him down with her car. She said her mind fogged and the street was dark and she had likely had too much wine with the man she went home with after we'd all gone to our own places to lie beside each other in bed and say nothing other than goodnight.

Impossible

Momma told Jimmy to watch out for the French leg of her curio cabinet next to the front door. He was clumsy, and on his way out and Jimmy kept catching his big, dumb foot and insisting he didn't know what she meant by French leg. Jimmy didn't know much about the French or anything else for that matter. She'd look at him and say it was French because it stuck out and was thin and was doing an ooh-la-la that other pieces of furniture didn't do.

He knew how much Momma loved her curio cabinet and all the little glass cats she kept inside but when we broke up he disrespected us and kicked it over before he slammed the door. That was the end of Momma's favorite cat. Its tail snapped. Grandma had given it to her a week before she died. It can't be fixed. It can't be glued together again, just like me and Jimmy if we decided to try again and I know we won't.

Jimmy started at me over breakfast. He said he didn't like the eagle and the flag on my chest. "You're overweight," he said, and "it was just wrong to do that to two national symbols, let alone one," because I not only wanted to show respect to America but my pride in the fact that's all I am, proud and free and so what?

He said I was so big I could be America. I didn't like that and threw a cup of hot coffee in his face. When we were being tender he used to say I was a lot of real estate and that was meant in a nice kind way, but when he left today he just said I spread bigger than Nebraska in a wind storm.

Now that he's gone, I want to know what I was doing with him. I wanted to know why he kept showering three times a day. He said he was greasy from the heat, but I could tell there was something else, something he wanted to wash away that wasn't me. He had a trailer parked in a vacant lot near the river, but he never hooked up his show or his sink and now that he's out of my life he's going to die of stink, but that don't take care of Momma. Momma's got a broken heart and a broken cat.

Miracles aren't supposed to happen. Those are the Lord's work. Glue don't count. If he glued the tail on the cat with the little sparkly eyes, the one Grandma gave Momma just before Grandma went to the Lord, there'd always be a line. A line is something no one should cross, especially when it is drawn and someone is asking for forgiveness. Jesus wouldn't be forgiving if someone crossed his line.

But after I picked up all the pieces of Momma's curios, I held that little cat in my arms and it seemed so small and helpless and needing my love and I had some left because Jimmy wasn't getting it no more and I set it back on the shelf with its tail beside it and held Momma in my arms as she cried herself to sleep. Momma didn't curse Jimmy like she could have thought he wasn't respecting us no more. She didn't ask the Lord to strike him down or send a tornado to carry off his mobile home. Instead, she just lay in my arms calling, "Come back little cat! Come back!" It wasn't pathetic. It was just sad. It was wanting something to be put right the way it once was and it was such a little thing.

So I drove up and down the backroads and figured I'd find Jimmy somewhere, either hanging out at his friend Dave's place or maybe in a ditch where filth like him belongs after what he all did to Momma's curio cabinet, and I finally found him. He saw me get out of the car and he smiled. Smiled. I mean, don't y'all think he'd have an ounce of contrition? But not Jimmy. He started coming around the front of the car, putting his dirty, greasy hands all over the hood even though the car was dirty and it probably didn't matter.

That's when I picked up Pa's pitchfork I brought it with me because Momma said as I was leaving the trailer, "Y'all gonna give that devil a piece of his own medicine," and I said, "Sure am," as the screen door closed behind me and I knew I had some justice to do. So when Jimmy comes toward me, smiling, with his arms wide open he doesn't see Pa's pitchfork so right through the passenger side window I stuck that bastard. He looked surprised. He said, "Baby? What's all this?" So I pulled it out and stuck him again and he fell. And just like I was bailing hay, I kept sticking him until he was shovelled into a ditch where he moaned and rolled over and went splash, face-first into the six inches of water in the gulley and I stood there until his legs stopped twitching and his ball cap came off and floated around his head.

"Did you get him?" Momma asked when I came home and turned on Family Feud and sat there watching it. She had picked up all the rare little pieces of her precious cat and I said, "Yep. He's dead as dead, but he didn't apologize. He didn't say 'I'm sorry,' not even one little bit. And it serves him right, and I just sat there the rest of the day watching but not really watching the TV because I knew I'd done something wrong by breaking a man's life but he'd gone and broken Momma's curio cabinet and I figured we were even.

In the morning I woke up early and looked at the curios and the cat was smiling and his eyes were twinkling even more than I remembered, and his tail was whole. It was attached just as I remembered it. First I thought Jimmy came in during the night with some glue but the door had been locked. No one had come in except maybe an angel or the hand of some mysterious heart and cured that little cat.

It's impossible but the little cat is whole again. Grandma would be happy because she said this country is about pursuing a more perfect kind of place. She's probably smiling down at us from the Lord's country and trying to tell us we can't go on feeling hurt by those who have hurt themselves and the path out of life or trailers or towns is full of broken things wanting forgiving and forgetting though I'm sure the cat with the sparkly little eyes remembers just as well as I do. I'm thinking if something breaks your heart enough something else comes along and mends because for every evil in the world, there's got to be a little bit of good though most of the time no one can see it unless they had little sparkly eyes. I know now I can mend it myself if I put my mind to it.

The Hands

Although her real estate agent could not say exactly when the salt-box cottage had been built, Gail was certain some clues to the past lay beneath layers of wallpaper in the front room. There had once been a fireplace in the over-papered main room and she imagined people gathered in its radiance to converse, spend quiet evenings together as they listened to the snap of old-growth maple in the flames, or dined at a long heavy table. The feet left dark circles on the wide-cut pine floorboards. She would hire a carpenter and a mason to rebuild her hearth.

First, the old wallpaper had to go. Layer after layer the paper loosened and gave way. Along with the crown work at the top of the room, someone painted a scroll of dolphins playing in the surf, an anomaly this far north.

The final layer had been a yellow print of petite sweetheart roses suspended in floating love knots. Someone thought them beautiful, but the longer Gail stared, the more the pattern reminded her of bodies washing ashore from a shipwreck, shapes floating face down in the surf, each looking for something they lost.

The brown handprints were troubling. They had palms and thin, delicate fingers of a woman's hand. Gail felt sick. Something terrible had happened in that room and the victim put a signature to her terror.

And their colour.

They had not been made by a playful child who, having been told he or she could draw on the walls before they were papered over. They were monochromatic brown and reminded her of a dried red rose she found pressed in the pages of a book in the attic. Blood if left to dry on paper, wallpaper, or fresh plaster, also fades to brown over time.

They sickened Gail who immediately attacked the handprints with a mixture of water and trisodium phosphate. She was going to fight back. She scored the surface with an old paper hanger's shredder. The hands were almost expunged as she felt a pang of grief because one or two left impressions of a lifeline and heart line on the wall. Determined, she filled the scoring with filler from the local hardware store and rolled on three coats of heavy-duty white latex paint, then called it a day.

In the morning, she was ready to give the room its new look, and by noon she had hung a fresh antique yellow print of daffodils. Happiness, she decided, could put fear and violence in the past.

She left the house to do her grocery shopping. She returned with the last bags from the car but let them fall from her hands. She gasped as she stared at the wall where the handprints bled through the plaster patches, the overpainting. Her name was indelible on the new wallpaper where smudged uncials and brown droplets, still warm and sticky to her touch, wept from every letter.

Flapjacks

The men who killed me believed they had to sacrifice a father's only son to save themselves from their sins. Who could blame them? They were simply following scripture. Scripture is a set of orders. Those who follow it believe they are doing good. They are certain violence is the right thing to do.

But it was my life.

No one asked if I was willing to give myself.

I was the lamb, the purity they sought to destroy to redeem them from their failings. I was only ten.

My parents brought me to the town of Mortimer when I was six years old. My father was hired to work in the new tractor factory. I started school in Mortimer. I loved the town though I was aware very early on the town did not love me or the other children of workers because we spoke a different language and ate foods and smelled of garlic and peppers people didn't understand. But the more I hung around the streets or played by myself on the riverbank or watched the trees bend to the breath of the wind or walked the dusty road from Main Street to our house on the edge of town, the more I felt the town was inside me, that it had become who I was becoming by growing up there.

Mortimer was built around a swift-flowing artery of the Mad River where the slow current became rapids. The rush of the water over mid-stream stones was ideal for turning the wheels of aw mill machinery. I loved to watch the eddies swirl and froth against the mid-stream stones. I marvelled at the way the shore grass submerged and began mermaid hair in the flow. The river was named for its wild and anguished race to arrive somewhere it didn't need to be. The Mad was loud the way water shouts so nothing can be heard over it. The sound where it hammered at the rusted mill wheel overpowered my ears.

My father stood smoking on the bridge one Sunday afternoon, and he turned to say something and I was sure he was offering me wisdom but I couldn't tell what he said. His voice was drowned in the air. As a family among those pushed aside by the center of the town – the factory workers whose names and languages were odd were silenced in every possible way, even by the river.

The newcomers were not meant to be heard or to hear each other. In the factory, talking was not permitted among the workers, and if they spoke to each other they would be docked pay. The penalty was doubled if they were caught speaking a language other than English. The foreman thought talk among the machine workers was a fomenting of revolution. But the men whispered and the machinery drowned them out and they understood each other as if they were hearing the voices of angels whose whispers were beyond the power of mere mortals to comprehend.

My mother tried to speak to the women she met in shops, but they would turn and ignore her and she would stand and wait, patiently, for the local women from the center of the town to finish their purchases and leave, and only then would she be served. In school, I was hushed and beaten if I so much as sighed. One day in a dry goods store my mother pointed at a skein of blue wool she fancied. The clerk sold her a bright green ball of yarn instead. My mother, however, was undaunted and made me a pair of socks that almost came up to my knee. I had them on the night I was murdered. That was how she identified my body.

My death took place behind one of the shops on the main street, an avenue named for the Duke of Wellington whose soldiers were exiled to woodland towns such as Mortimer as a reward for having killed other men in battle. Having murdered once they wanted to take their rage out on the land when they arrived. They swung their axes not merely to fell a tree but with the intent to murder whatever stood in their way.

My father told me that our family had not been soldiers. Our family had been the battlefield. Each time an invading army marched through the towns and farmyards to burn the house, the barn, and carry off the livestock, someone would hitch a sick bull to a cart and either force it to trudge toward the invaders or away from them. Sometimes the man of the family would be conscripted to fight for a cause he didn't believe in. Other times, the man would be murdered, the ox confiscated to feed hungry troops, and the woman with her children would hitch the harness around her shoulders and pull the wagon with her meagre belongings wherever she thought she could be safe.

The lumbermen arrived first in Mortimer and tried to assert their claim to supremacy. They were French from Quebec. Some had served in Napoleon's army and carried the sting and anger of defeat with them. They claimed they were doing the Lord's work by making it easier for the next wave to come along and beat the victors into the dust. They built a sawmill on the riverbank, and then a competing sawmill on the other bank so anyone who tried to settle the town-site went out of their minds with the agonizing grating of saw teeth gnawing and gasping on the hardwood. And if the mills fell silent when the river froze and the logs could not be floated downstream, people would hear echoes of snaps and shots of axes ringing out like gunfire followed by the tortured scream of trees falling from their stand.

As the trees became scarce, the lumbermen saw their survival as a matter of diversification. They built sugar shacks on their woodlots. Each spring they would collect the maple sap, drop by drop, as it slowly filled pails hung from spigots driven into the trunks of trees. When each bucket was even a quarter full, the precious, clear liquid would be collected in a large kettle set to boil inside the shack on fires stoked with oak boughs and white-hot cords of the lesser woods such as birch and elm. For miles around Mortimer, I could smell the sickly-sweet aroma of the sap being reduced as clouds of steam rose from the shacks and caught the rush of March wind.

A gallon of clear, watery sap reduced to a pint of maple syrup after twelve hours on a slow boil. The longer the sap 'sugared off,' the darker it would become. Amber was the staple of the syrups, but the deep, thick brown syrup often called "tar" or "pitch" was highly prized. If the dark syrup were allowed to boil for another day or two in a smaller kettle, it would thicken into maple butter. My mother bought a tiny jar of it, though it cost two days of my father's wages and she had to explain where the money had been wasted and he was angry until he tasted the delicacy. Maple butter is ambrosia on freshly baked brown bread. I was permitted to try some and I thought I had heaven in my mouth.

The farmers, mostly Scots who had been displaced from their land on the other side of the ocean, purchased the denuded forests. They had no means of demarcating their boundaries, so the stumps they pulled were tilted on their sides to create fences and prove ownership of their plots. As they turned over the soil, many fell sick with a malady they called mesmalaria. Their children ran fevers and died. But the farmers were undaunted. Each spring they tilled their fields and sowed the land with feed grains, raised hogs that could be butchered and cured in maple wood smoke from the cuttings left behind by the lumbermen, and for a while, they became the dominant group in Mortimer.

When an east-west crossroad was cut through the bush so the farmers could have ready access to their markets in the city, the townsmen finally gained the upper hand. They built hotels where auctioneers could stay as the farmers auctioned their cattle to be butchered in the city. Mortimer's sawmills were soon replaced by grist mills driven by the same river that had drowned out the axe cracks and the cries of splitting trunks a generation before.

And as the town grew, it attracted three churches: a Catholic parish attended by the lumbermen who came from Quebec in the failed belief there was no end to the trees they could fell, a Presbyterian kirk where the congregation was mostly dour farmers with little tolerance for popish behaviour and idolatry, and a Methodist house of worship that opened its doors to the businessmen of the town who believe they could do good for others but did little good when the opportunity arose. We didn't have a church. My father would intone prayers by candlelight and would tell us God was listening to every word.

The Methodist minister was a man named Chisholm who quickly gained a reputation as a person of sound judgment, and even temper, but faint-hearted action. He built the school but delayed hiring a teacher for it as long as he could to keep the Presbyterians and Catholics away, neither of whom, he believed, should be permitted to have an education unless they supported learning with cold, hard cash. He declined the townsfolk's offer to declare him mayor. He talked the townspeople out of holding elections for fear there would be violence at the polls. There were stories that voting in other towns was done with the persuasive assistance of axe handles.

But despite Chisholm's efforts to keep the peace the feuding began.

There were drunken brawls in the hotel's beverage room when a Presbyterian Scot said something a French Catholic disliked. The fight was carried out into the streets. A dress shop belonging to a Methodist elder who was known for being outspoken was torched before the lumbermen fled or took refuge in the Catholic church, forcing the priest to say mass in the dark hours of the morning.

The tipping point in the war between the farmers and the lumbermen happened one night when the loggers came into town and got drunk in a saloon operated by another Quebecer, Pierre Tardif. The Presbyterians forbade liquor but were known to drink, and the Methodists would not drink at all. On the night in question, the loggers stumbled from the hotel. One of them was carrying an axe handle. Another had a pot lid lifter from his sugar shack. The farmers immediately armed themselves with anything they could find. The stage was set for a battle.

I was sleepless the spring night I was murdered.

My mother had fallen ill. She was prone to headaches that would paralyze her. She would scream with the pain in her face and the side of her head, but no matter how loud her sufferings grew we could not afford a doctor. The payment would have cost my father a week's wages and the next week we would have gone hungry. He was paid just enough in the factory for us to rent our two-room house, which consisted of a kitchen and my parent's bed on one side of a thin wall, and my small room on the other., What was left bought after paying for the roof over our heads was enough for potatoes, salted meat, and bread.

The druggist, Mr. Sinclair, knew of my mother's affliction and took pity on her, perhaps having heard her cries when he was out for a Sunday buggy ride, or maybe from local gossip who thought her pain was a sign of insanity. Just after midnight, my father could not take her misery anymore and told me to go to the apothecary and ask for some laudanum to make my mother sleep.

On the road into town, I could hear the brawling. The men on both sides were cursing at each other, shouting. The Methodists had drawn their shades. The Presbyterians were in a pitched battle with the Catholics.

I knocked on the druggist's door in the hope he would hear me and dispense the medication. I knocked at least five times on the glass and when I turned around, both the Catholic lumbermen and the Presbyterian farmers had stopped fighting.

Men on both sides were armed with axe handles and other implements, brake shafts from their wagons, shovels – anything they could use to harm each other. A few of them began to smoke.

Mr. Sinclair would not answer his door. I stared at the gathering as their leaders – Lebecque and McGraw – were talking to each other in hushed tones and pointing at me. I decided to run between the stores but the aggressors came around from my left and my right. I was alone and surrounded. That is when they struck me. The first blow to my mouth.

The last thing I can recall of my life was the taste of my blood in my mouth and the feeling I had no top to my head. And even though I was dead, they kept hitting me, each blow harder than the last until my skull spread in the alleyway dirt and a sickening feeling rose from my stomach and nothing mattered anymore.

Someone must have looked out their window. Someone must have shouted that murder had been done. My body was taken to the Methodist church because the story about my death says the lamps were lit that night and burned until sunrise.

I was identified by my green stockings. They had slipped down around my ankles as I tried to run. My father is said to have lifted my mother in his arms and walked to the church from the edge of town when a messenger arrived at our small house around three in the morning to break the news to my parents.

When my mother saw what they had done, there was nothing for her to hold, nothing to cradle in her arms, no head to swaddle in bandages, or forehead to caress and weep over.

All she could do was scream through the pain already torturing her. "What have you done to my son? What have the monsters done to you?" And no one could understand a word because everything she said was in a language no one spoke.

I know what happened.

During their brawl, Lebecque and McGraw were on the verge of killing each other. Both men paused, stood up, and embraced. The men on the opposing sides saw this and they fell motionless and awestruck as if they were witnessing a miracle.

And why shouldn't they experience the hand of the Almighty? It was the moment the town needed if it was going to survive. It was the hand of an angel reaching out to them and calling a truce.

As they whispered to each other and I kept banging on Mr. Sinclair's door, frightened for my life and desperate to get home with the medicine to help my mother, I saw them speaking.

The moment I was free of this life I knew what they said. They agreed to end their hostilities. They agreed the battles, according to the Holy Scriptures, the words of the one thing they held in common, declared that a sacrifice had to be made, and an only son, a firstborn's blood would purify the putrid streets. I was the chosen one. The lamb for the slaughter could not be permitted to get away.

If I had survived, the battles would have continued. There would be nothing left of Mortimer. And as the two leaders made their way to the back of Sinclair's Apothecary, they decided how the ritual killing would take place. It had to be done properly. It had to be done in the eyes of the Lord or the sacrifice would have no purpose and no lasting power to rectify the damnation haunting the town. Those who oversaw my end simply bashed in my skull, each side agreeing to the same number of blows. No one was entitled to a stroke more or could deliver a stroke less than what had been agreed to be fair. I never knew who issued the fatal hit.

As the townsmen, the lumbermen, and the farmers sat in the Methodist chapel and awaited the arrival of the Reverend Chisholm, They said my death had to have a lasting effect on the town so as brothers forever they'd be sworn by a blood bond and that would be commemorated annually by the breaking of bread and the sacrament of blood from the trees. They would meet once each year for a Lord's Breakfast, not a Lord's supper because by the time they reached their decision in the chapel the last stars were receding from the sky in anticipation of the first cock-crowing at the first grey-green sunlight etched across the eastern horizon. When everyone was assembled in the chapel – lumbermen, farmers, townsmen – they locked the doors behind them, sealing the factory workers out – and brokered their treaty.

They called upon Reverend Chisholm to preside over the settlement of their grievances, and all present signed the document in blood, pledging they would never divulge the details of what transpired that night. That document was buried somewhere in the town, perhaps laid to rest beneath the steps of the town hall or dug into the freshly turned earth of my grave.

When the meeting was over and the angry mob of factory workers outside dispersed, Chisholm packed his wife, daughter, and their belongings in an ox cart and left the town while everyone went home to sleep safely in their beds with their window blinds pulled down. Chisholm would never say, even on his deathbed, what transpired during the meeting on that summer night.

No one was ever charged with my murder, but the following year, on the anniversary of the deed, the lumbermen and the farmers appeared before dawn in the main street of the town and set up long trestle tables. Farmers and foresters alike hauled wagons brimming with what they took from the world – maple syrup from the remaining stands of ancient growth trees, sacks of flour, trays of eggs, and rounds of butter they mixed into a batter and cooked on grills fired by chips and shards of wood.

They dragged chairs from the town hall, the new library, the hotel, and their own homes, and set them up twelve to each side of a table. The wives of the loggers and the farmers rolled up their sleeves and with wooden spoons mixed the ingredients into a flesh-coloured batter that bubbled on the grills signifying it was time to flip them on the other side. Jugs of maple syrup were set in the middle of each trestle. Pots of mapled baked beans boiled over open fires. Cast iron griddles heaped with maple sausages sizzled as the dawn rose. They washed every mouthful down with milk, pure and white. They celebrated their union over broken, unleavened bread that was my body and the rendered sap of maples that was my blood.

That is how the festival began.

Flapjacks put Mortimer on the map. Visitors flock to the town for one day every year. Then the window blinds are drawn and the streets are empty as if no one lives there. But on the morning when the concord began, when peace finally came to the community, farmers, lumbermen, and townsfolk paused before the first mouthful. They did not say grace. Instead, they joined hands, raised their eyes to the sky, and for a moment and asked silently for forgiveness, wondering if my spirit was present and presiding over their bounty in eternal peace.

The Printer of St. Barthlélemay

My family's printing shop was the reason we lived in the middle of the Bayou. The geography I once called my home was little more than a rise from the tangles of weeds growing from the briny water. There were only two trees in town, two ancient cypresses draped in flowing Spanish Moss, the trunks and branches cloaked in the sadness of loss. The trees bent like widows who had rent their clothing and now hung from the boughs in a perpetual aura of grief.

Aside from a small store and the print shop, which locals approached in airboats, there wasn't much to the place. I learned to work an ancient press and became very adept at typesetting. The Printer's Devil in the shop was named Scratch. Scratch was old, and he'd been a Printer's Devil a long time. The Devil in a print shop is the assistant to the whole operation, pulling sheets, fetching flagons of water, and inking the cold type. I have no idea where my father found him, but there was a murky depth to his brown eyes. He said he could play steel guitar, but we never heard a note from him. The three of us would spend our days in my father's shop, pulling handbills and parish notices we'd hang on the porch posts and the cypresses. By noon, I'd be drenched in sweat. Printing is as demanding as paving, but far more physical. The heat in midsummer tormented me. Scratch was immune.

For as long as I could remember, Scratch worked for my father, and I never saw him being paid, although my mother always put a full plate in front of him. He never gave us an idea how long he'd been at his job until one afternoon I broke my silence and asked him outright.

He fell silent, and didn't say another word for the remainder of the day, except for when we were locking up.

"Someone said you were from North aways?" I said. "Memphis, to be precise, and you were hiding out in St. Barthélemay's print shop because you murdered a man. That was the story, anyway." The facts behind his life didn't make sense. Many were etched in history.

Scratch fell silent and had a vicious smile on his face, not a nice, happy smile, but the look of someone who knows about something someone has done and is prepared to use it against them.

"Look to your doing, boy, " he said. "Look to your doing. Your father wants to pull copies of this job and have it done tomorrow."

Under his breath, Scratch left me feeling he was somewhere else. He muttered so many quiet thoughts, I felt I couldn't trust him with the truth. "I am a slave to time and life," he said.

"Do you ever wish you were a free man/"

"Who says I'm not? What you need to learn, kid, is everyone is free in some way. Even the poor souls I saw on auction blocks were free, though maybe only in their souls. I'm a Printer's Devil. I chose to be a Printer's Devil. It is my calling."

On the Northern rise, there'd once been a parish church, a small town, and a ladies' school but all the salt marshes wiped away the parish. One night there was a hurricane. Rising tides and floodwaters change a place, reorganize the landscape, and say to the world, "You are only what you are as long as I permit you to exist."

The more I thought about Scratch's mutterings, the more I wanted to escape the place and my moment in the world, and be someone somewhere else. So when the night finally settled on St. Barthélemay, I got up from my bed and left to find the world.

There were two rises in the road through the Bayou. The one on which the town once sat ran through a marsh where the mosquitoes were so bad during the summer, people didn't talk to one another. The foundations of the long-lost church poked through the stinking shallows.

The road south was smooth. About twenty minutes from the gulf, I felt the cool breezes, heard the cries of gulls, and realized I was standing on the remains of sand bar. I had never been to the Southern Rise, but on that Lord's Day, when I ran away from home at the age of sixteen, I took the Southern road to the edge of the Bayou. The sun wasn't up yet, and the night had not died. The crickets were mad with the litanies of their hind legs. I heard a steel guitar being played with such incredible beauty, I thought I was hearing the music of heaven. A man in his forties was squatting in the dust as he played. When he stopped strumming, the insects fell silent. He emerged behind me from the ground fog.

"Sit down, kid, take a load off. Where you going?"

"Memphis," I said, but I added I wasn't sure.

"Well, you're sure now. Memphis is the other way. Go north past the rise ahead. Go around Lake Ponchartrain, and be careful not to get too near the shore because the lake is full of gators who are bigger than the ones out here, and even hungrier. When you reach New Orleans, grab the Triangle Line north. Memphis is about seven hours."

"Do you know anyone there?" I asked.

"No one still alive, " he replied. I killed someone in Memphis and had to leave. You can't stay too long in Memphis. I can't go back, though I doubt they're looking for me anymore. It's a wicked city, so no one missed a sinner or two."

"By the way," he added, "my name is Scratch. I have something for you. Years ago on this road, right here to be precise, there used to be another road to a long-drowned plantation. I met a man at this crossroads. I asked him what his name was. He replied, 'You've always known me. I'm willing to make a trade. I'll give you a gift but you'll have to give me a gift as well.' He handed me this case that contained Claudia, my steel guitar. He said, 'Go ahead, you already know what you want to play and how to play it. Every note is already inside you. All you have to do is set it free – you're an artist.' And then he was gone, leaving me with this," Scratch said as he patted the figure eight of his instrument's body. "I know you're not the musician type. Just looking at you tells me you're a man of words. My gift to you is in this case, " he said, as he handed me a small suitcase with a handle on top. "You will give the words every fibre of your soul."

And with that, Scratch was gone, and there I was standing in the middle of nowhere with an aged Underwood in its own small coffin. Scratch wanted me to be a writer. Maybe he had aspirations once. Maybe the long-dead men he had known were calling out to him from the battlefields of time, asking if he would find someone to tell their story, so they could be mourned and remembered.

I turned in the road and headed north, and when I looked back, there was no sign of a crossroad at all. In New Orleans, I considered hopping a boxcar, but an old timer in the railyard told me I'd get robbed, so I took a seat in the mail carriage of the Triangle Line.

Memphis was far from welcoming. The Mississippi nuzzles the city. I got a cheap hotel near the station, so if I murdered someone, I could tell Scratch what it felt like to make a quick getaway.

About four days into my stay, I found a roll of bills on the sidewalk (OK, I had just robbed an old man at knifepoint) and was eating scrambled eggs and coffee when I struck up a conversation with my server Nuala. She had dark brown eyes. We walked that night along the river, the Mississippi that is the modern-day equivalent of the Nile, behind warehouses and hobo encampments, and she said she liked me. That's how we began. Two months later, we were married.

Life with Nuala was happy enough. We got a little apartment and began our lives together. Her uncle Charlie was the only member of Nuala's family to acknowledge us. One day when Nuala was at the diner, I asked Charlie for twenty bucks to help out with the rent. He refused. So I went to a drawer in the kitchen and found a sharp boning knife. When I came back into the room, he looked at me and said, "I know what you're going to do, so why do it for such a measly amount? Why not fifty or seventy-five?"

"You got that kind of cash on you, Charlie?" When he said no, I stabbed him ten times in his skinflint heart because that's what Scratch would have done. I'm sure Charlie was dead, but just to make doubly sure, I slit his throat. He just lay there looking at me like I had a question I wanted to ask, but he couldn't answer it, at least not in that condition. I packed up my Underwood, and was gone from Memphis before Nuala could return from work. The city of Memphis, named for the ancient capital of Egypt, had been my strange, dark place. The words poured out of me. I had no control over them. Novels, plays, short stories – everything that ever touched my life – pleaded to be proclaimed to the world. I felt I had to return the life I would take from the world, so I poured it into my words. People die in silence, but writers live in it. They capture the voices of the world and hush them into the winterscape of the page. I packaged up my words and sent them off as manuscripts to the publishers in New York and Boston. After killing Charlie, I hid out in the world of the rural poor, working by day in a lumber mill in Arkabutia and preaching in a little Baptist church by the lake on Sundays. I wondered what had become of my art. Had I captured my silence in an absurd butterfly net where thoughts break their wings?

One night, I caught a bus into the city. I went to the vestibule of our old apartment to see if there were responses to all my submissions. All the publishers wanted my work. I didn't know what to do. Was it a police trap intended to draw me in? I wasn't sure. I was about to grab a seat on the bus out when I ran into a young woman who had lived down the hall. I asked if anyone was looking for the man who once lived here with Nuala.

"Looking for you? Not likely. Nuala died of old age last year. The diner where she worked is long gone. Anyone who thought they knew the scoundrel who killed the poor girl's uncle is long gone. Nuala lived alone and died alone last year. She waited seventy years, and not a word was heard about her husband. It was like he was swallowed up by time and turned to dust."

I had nowhere else to go, so I returned to St. Barthlélemay. Scratch handed me a stack of newspapers and magazines with headlines that asked where the great Southern writer was hiding. When I walked into the print shop, my father looked up from his inking and glared at me.

"Look what the Devil dragged in. Where the hell have you been? I haven't seen you in the Devil knows how long."

"No, that can't be right. I was only gone a matter of weeks. I met Scratch out on the road through the Southern Rise. Almost eighty years went by." I fired back in defence.

"You don't look a day past sixteen to us, boy," my father said.

"Scratch gave me my typewriter."

"The hell he did. Liar! Scratch has been here the whole time. Hasn't missed an hour as long as I've known him. Put on your apron and get back to work."

Scratch stood there smiling.

"There's a lot of life in you, kid. People like us who meet at the crossroads never die. We just go on doing whatever our souls ask."

The Lay-By

They hadn't planned to break their trip back from a shallow bass inlet where good fish played in and out of the rocky shadows and the warm sandy bottom, but the outboard was running out of gas. There was an island Od had heard about where a woman named Cici had a boater lay by in a blind cove where they could pull in and replenish their boats and their throats if they'd gone out too far for the perfect catch. Local talk said she had an old Texaco pump that went ding as it flowed and the spillage left gasoline rainbows at the footings of her dock. And she sold beer but Od wasn't sure it would be cold because there'd been some discussion about whether she still had electricity. "How the hell would she pay for it," he'd wondered.

Artie was sure the tank had been brimful, and he turned as the engine dropped into a lower rev and the boat glided toward Cici's dock. He thought they ought to be careful of her. Cici saw them coming from a mile away and met them as they pulled in.

"Chuffing dry?" she said. Not hello. Not howdy or good day. She was pointing out the obvious. To her, men were pigs. "I'll fill her up so why don't you boys grab a beer from the cooler and stare at the water."

A few minutes later, as Cici approached Dave and Od and Artie, the boys were into their second cans. Od said he didn't mind that it was warm. "Best damned beer I've had in ages."

"Who owns the boat?" Od raised a hand and nodded. "Did you know your spark plug is shot and probably the alternator?"

"It was working fine on the way in."

"Well, they don't make plugs like that anymore and the ones you have aren't going to last to get you home. Say, how about some Jack? Something stronger? Where you headed?"

Od said, "Mean's Bay. It's about five miles around the other side of that far island there. Can't see it from here, but it's out there. And no thanks. Boating laws and regulations. But Artie and Dave?" His companions nodded.

"Yep," said Cici, "gas can run you out here. Overheads. Distances. The cost of doing business if you're out for a good day's fishing." By this time, she was pouring a tumbler of whisky each for Artie and Dave although she knew it was illegal to operate a motorboat while inebriated. "Funny, between here and there, lots of boats are lying on the bottom. They go down real easy and it is starting to get dark." Artie and Dave thought it was funny. They thought Cici was making a joke about being swallowed by Georgian Bay in the dark. They snorted. Od looked at them. They were turning into pigs, not just in their behaviour but in their appearance. Their faces were growing round, their noses shorted into their heads, and pink bristles started to appear on their chins.

"How much?" asked Od. "And guys, pull yourselves together."

"The gas? The beers, the Jack? Oh, hard to say. And the mechanic's work of investigation I had to do on your machine there. You can't be too careful. Five hundred and we're square. I don't take cheques or credit cards. Cash only."

"Look lady," Od snapped, "we've been out on the water all day. We're sunburned. And you don't carry a wad of cash with you to lure a fish."

"Should. Some fish can't be caught but they can be bought."

"Do you have cellphone service out here? Maybe I can call my wife and she can get a water taxi to run out here with some money, though I'm not paying you five brownies to get off your island."

"Suit yourself," Cici said. She turned, walked to the dock, and undid the mooring ropes. Before Od could reach them, the boat had drifted and washed ashore, returning them to the same spot from which they thought they had departed.

They thought they were happy. Cici had what seemed an unlimited supply of beer and rye and she doled it out to the boys. Artie and Dave had, indeed, turned into pigs.

Od looked at them in disgust. They'd always been that way, and he thought it was because most men are pigs. It is ingrained in them. It is part of their temperament. Now and then as Cici passed them, they would make a lewd remark to her and to placate the two she would empty a pail of garbage on the ground of their pen, while Od sat on a rocky point staring toward the passage. The boys didn't need to say junk like that to her, but they were the type of men who lost control of their manners when waitresses tried to serve them in restaurants. Od felt so ashamed of them then and even more ashamed of them now. When he passed the boys the next day, they were lying on a sloping rockface in the sun. They were naked and asleep – drunk as skunks – and their mouths were open like a string of fish someone had caught the day before, their bodies stinking, and their eyes round and glassy, staring at nothing.

Od's wife was waiting out there, somewhere, though by now they would have found the empty boat and assumed that all three had drowned. Death by misadventure. Cici kept assuring him that life on her island wasn't so bad. Legend had it that previous inhabitants had lived long and wonderful lives there, free from care and worries, and she had a warehouse full of well-aged bourbon that a bootlegger had stashed on the island eighty years before and that her elixir went as down smooth as water on the limestone shoreline.

But Od was certain his wife would be sitting at her quilting rack to ease her grief, stitching a coverlet that was intended to keep them warm on nights when they stayed after the summer season was over to enjoy the quiet. And Od would weep and whisper under his breath, "Please find me. I am still here." The coverlet was eighty shades of blue to remind them of the view of Georgian Bay from their cottage window, not just in the morning, but at all times of the day and was just large enough to cover the double bed that had been a wedding present from his parents and where they had spent the first night of their lives together, vowing never to lose hope in the other.

Archivist

Visitors must sign an oath not to set any fires. The reading room is always cold. The clock hammers in a minute as if it just sold another parcel of time. A reader leans forward and whispers his request. I know where everything is stored.

"I want to know about tragedy," the man in the tweed jacket says in a hush. "Sadness, loss, grief. You name it. I need to know more about it."

I look at him as if he has lost his mind. Yes, I know where it is but finding it will take time. There are no fast ways to fathom what breaks the heart but at least an archive is the last place touched by time.

Grief. Tragedy. Drama. Novels. Letters. A daily newspaper. Perhaps trade publications.?

David Hume would have a field day inside my head. Life blends so easily with printed matter. He can't possibly want it all. Memory can't unsee what is seen.

I can't forget telephone numbers, serial numbers, titles, authors, and the number on the side of the fire truck the night my home burned. It was Monday, January 29, 1977. I was five years, three months, and twenty days old.

The policeman, 5362, knelt beside me and said I was the only one who got out alive.

I brought the first of one hundred carts from the stacks but the man probably heard the sirens, but had to be somewhere, or hadn't time to wait for it all.

Eleanor

Her father never hung Mexican fly strips because he believed the insects were tiny demons and chased them around the house with a fly swatter. The walls, especially in the summer when the barnyard was ripe, were splattered with splotches of legs and wings. When her mother tried to rub them off with a rag and Dutch Cleanser, her father shook the woman violently by the wrist and insisted that leaving the bodies, like writing on the wall from the Old Testament, would serve as a warning to other flies, though the admonitions never worked and the house filled up with the insects day after day until Eleanor found it impossible to sleep even when she pulled a pillow over her head.

Now that she was out on her own with "No hope of ever going back," her father's words, she hung up a Mexican fly strip beside the desk in the room Bob found for her on Curtis Street with Mrs. Carlisle so the insects wouldn't buzz annoyingly when Eleanor went on Facebook. Bob was her rescuer. The people at the truck stop agreed there was something wrong with the way her father hit her and hit her hard as Eleanor screamed she was being abducted. Mrs. Carlisle was her guardian. They told Eleanor she was safe but could no longer be Eleanor Bane.

Mrs. Carlisle recorded her conversations with Eleanor's permission. Eleanor wanted to make sure that even if something happened to her others would know what she had been through. Mrs. Carlisle assured Eleanor that nothing would happen to her, that she and Bob and the organization would do everything they could to protect her. The organization gave girls like Eleanor their freedom. It gave them their lives, taught them to read and write, and how to become part of the world they had been denied. The struggle for such young women was not merely leaving the homes and families they had known but leaving behind the identities they had been given. Many of the girls were only eighteen or nineteen. Bob wondered how Eleanor had lasted to twenty-three.

"No one wanted to marry me," she said. "They told me I was worthless and would make a poor wife. I had to watch as the girls I knew when I was younger became the sixth or seventh wives of men who were old enough to be my grandfathers. I told everyone I did not want children. They inspected me. There may have been some reason why I could not bear children. The old men said I was barren."

Bob told her that out here, in the real world, that didn't matter. Children were her choice. Eleanor had trouble understanding that, but she trusted Bob. Bob was her friend but he wasn't on Facebook. Mrs. Carlisle wasn't on Facebook either. Bob said his line of work didn't permit him to have social media pages and that Mrs. Carlisle flew beneath the radar, whatever that was, so girls like Eleanor would stand a chance once they broke free and got out into the world.

Eleanor wasn't sure what social media was. It sounded like a party. When she asked Bob if Facebook was a party he smiled and said it had been built for that but now it was often a dangerous neighborhood where people attacked one another, and Eleanor didn't want to be attacked anymore. She wasn't permitted to post pictures of herself which was fine because she didn't have any. Her hair had been dyed brown and cut short so they told her she looked like a pixie, and she wasn't sure what a pixie was either. Her name was Mindy now. Mindy Smith.

That's what it said on her name tag from Happy Land where she put her dyed hair in a brown net fitted over with a wrap-around brim to shade her eyes instead of a full brown baseball cap. If Mindy thought she recognized someone from her past, Bob showed her the way to drop her chin, hunch her shoulders, and look away. The boys on the job who joked with her got to wear full baseball caps. Mindy Smith's job was to keep the floors swept and mopped and to unload cartons of burgers and plastic bags of fries as the line cooks ran out. Eleanor didn't mind. Being someone else most of the week was a relief. She was busy and useful and Mr. Gallard who owned the restaurant told her she was diligent. That meant focused. He showed his gratitude by handing Mindy a cheque that Mrs. Carlisle would deposit into an account for

Eleanor so that when all the fuss blew over there'd be a nest egg, like a robin's, waiting for her so she could start a life where she didn't have to look over her shoulder. At the end of each day, Eleanor returned to her room when Mrs. Carlisle came to pick her up.

"We have to practice discretion," Mrs. Carlisle said. "Even though you are over the age of majority," whatever that meant, "we still brought you across state lines and because we're out of state they may come for you. The laws are different here than where you were," Mrs. Carlisle said. "The Children are looking for you and they won't give up until they find you and drag you back whether you want to be dragged back or not."

Facebook was full of faces but it was a lonely place. The Children didn't permit her to have Facebook but she had heard some of the girls in the compound giggling about it behind their hands so when Eleanor arrived at Mrs. Carlisle's house she asked if she could have Facebook and Mrs. Carlisle said, "Sure," because there was an old laptop kicking around that ought to do the trick and she sat down and taught Eleanor how to go online.

Eleanor giggled because the only thing she'd ever seen online was a fish her brother Roger caught in the creek back home before their father renamed him Isaac and wouldn't permit him to wear a hat when they worked in the fields. She didn't have any friends on Facebook except for the boy in Nigeria who wanted to marry her. She wasn't sure he was sincere and she told him she didn't have the money to fly him over so they could proceed with the necessary steps before matrimony. Maybe someday but not right now. Then he stopped being her friend. Making friends was difficult.

Learning to read was even harder. Mrs. Carlisle took pity on her one day and taught Eleanor how to sign her name so she could make bona fide applications for work. Eleanor didn't know what bona fide meant. It sounded slightly evil but she sensed Mrs. Carlisle meant well. The letters looped around each other like tangled vines in the weeds beside the stream back home.

When the flies came into Eleanor's room, Mrs. Carlisle gave her a Mexican fly strip and Eleanor thanked her and said she learned a lot about them by watching them die slowly. Mrs. Carlisle was surprised but not surprised. Eleanor explained that when she lived on a farm everything was about life and death and the things that die seldom stand a chance against the things that live. The Lord Almighty did not distinguish who or what should survive because everything was in His hands and most of the time His fist was clenched because He was a task-master Almighty who made people do His bidding or he'd smite them and they would bide no more. Eleanor told Mrs. Carlisle the story of her father and how he had driven his family beyond the reach of God in his pursuit of holiness only to bring them back, closer, and closer, to the nearness of the Lord because He must be obeyed as one obeys an earthly father no matter what.

The summer Eleanor was ten her earthly father came in from the cornfield late one hellfire of an afternoon. He hadn't worn his hat and had been working in the sun since dawn. His bald head was sunburnt and blazing red, although Eleanor wasn't sure she could say something was blazing on account of blazing being associated with you- know-where down there as she pointed to the floor. Her father told the family he had a vision. The Lord had called to him.

Eleanor wasn't sure there had been a voice.

The hogs had been restless and noisy all morning because an oil company was fracking nearby and the ground shook and shifted and part of the cornfield toppled sideways and fell into a hollow in the ground just before the pump water turned a filthy colour that was probably the work of you-know-who as she pointed to the floor again.

Her father held up a glass of the water that had been clear and tasty the day before and pointing to it hollered at Eleanor and her mother that they had poisoned the Lord's blessing with their blood. Eleanor wasn't sure what he meant.

"We must leave this place of sin. We must seek out our kind so that we may be cleansed."

Mrs. Carlisle said, "Go on. This is interesting," and set a glass of lemonade in front of Eleanor as they sat at the kitchen table. Eleanor thanked her and said her father used to hit her if she went on, but Mrs. Carlisle insisted she wouldn't hit her.

When her father came in from the corn, Eleanor's mother was sure her husband was suffering from sunstroke and told him he needed to wear a hat but he replied that he would never cover his head in reverence for the Lord because God's light touched his brain clear through his skull and wrapped its fingers around his thoughts until he realized the Lord Almighty had called the family to leave the farm as soon as

47

they could pack up only their clothing because they were heading west to join the Sons of Melchizedek and practice a new way of life. This had happened to her father before and when they picked up and left they always returned because the ways of man were a disappointment no matter how godly his fair creatures – and that didn't include flies – tried to be.

When Eleanor was eight, her family joined a group of the faithful where the women were instructed to wear long dresses no matter how hot the day was and set their hair up in an up-sweep above their eyes as if an angel lifted their womanly elegance from their foreheads so they could look unto the Lord above and feel His power and know His wrath. Eleanor's mother had not been happy because Eleanor's father wanted his wife and children, including Sadie who was only two, to obey his solemn commands. Crying was considered disobedience.

Eleanor took three long sips of lemonade and continued. Something happened to Sadie. Her mother wouldn't say what. Either the baby had fallen ill or she had cried after her father commanded her to obey him but after that, Sadie was gone without explanation. She asked if that was being inconsiderate and Mrs. Carlisle agreed that it most certainly was. Soon after the baby's disappearance, the family returned from the Sons of Gabriel to the family hog farm and Eleanor had to work twice as hard because the county was trying to take the land for back taxes and Eleanor's father was being charged with cruelty to animals because he'd walked away from his livestock and left the hogs and a cow to fend for themselves. The cow was caught several farms away but the hogs didn't do well because they were penned up.

As she and her mother dragged the hogs from the mud of the barnyard where they had fused with the land, the sacred land as her mother called it, Eleanor bent over and was sick from the smell. That's why she asked Mrs. Carlisle not to serve her bacon for breakfast after her guardian put a hearty plate in front of her the morning after Bob dropped her at her safe house. Mrs. Carlisle made great eggs. Her secret was a little bit of garlic powder. Eleanor told her they tasted wonderful but asked if her guardian was just a little bit afraid of the you-know-who down you-know-where who had something to do with garlic but Eleanor wasn't sure what. Mrs. Carlisle said no because her mother had been born in the south of France where everyone loves garlic and would eat it no matter what. Eleanor told her the eggs were better than a boiled potato.

"Is that all you ever got for breakfast?" and Eleanor replied un-huh, especially after her father's vision in the cornfield that sent them to live with the Children of Melchizedek.

Did Mrs. Carlisle know who Melchizedek was? Mrs. Carlisle nod-ded but Eleanor told her anyways. He was the angel who came to visit Lot and Lot's wife who turned to a pillar of salt for not obeying her husband, and M – she wasn't permitted to say his name too often – came to visit Lot and his family because he was going to destroy the wicked cities of Sodom and Gomorrah. Mrs. Carlisle agreed. Eleanor continued that the Children, better than the Sons because sons expect something and children just need to be seen and not heard and most of the time not seen at all, was ready to lay down their lives to destroy the wickedness of the cities, especially if they had railway stations and large office towers where wicked things happened.

"Like what?" Mrs. Carlisle asked.

Oh, just about everything wicked. I don't know everything that's wicked because I was not permitted to read or write and Bob says that's a disadvantage in this world and I have to weigh the pros with the cons, whatever they are, and just dive in and read and write and catch up from the ten years I was shut off from the world. The com-pound where the Children lived was lovely. There were mountains off in the distance. The summers were cooler, the winters were harder. Sadie caught sick with something and even though we prayed she went to Heaven to be with Jesus. I am frightened for her though.

"Why?" asked Mrs. Carlisle.

Eleanor stared out the kitchen window at the backyard and replied that Sadie didn't know how to read or write either and what would hap-pen if she went to Heaven to be with Jesus and she had to sign in or fill in a job application? There'd be no one to teach her unless Eleanor showed up and she didn't want to do that because there's more to life than I thought possible. I never dreamed there were streets with cars on them. I never dreamed there were expressways and shopping malls and Happy Arches where people could walk up to the counter and choose whatever they wanted from a menu of nutritious offerings with recom-mended food guidelines posted on the tiled wall though no one ever bothered to read them. I want to go into an office tower. I want to get on a train and go somewhere because they're like Facebook. They exist without anyone knowing they are there, just like I always thought of the Lord Almighty existing and no one realizing He was there right beside us as we worked in the fields without our hats on and only put on our scarves or caps as a sign of reverence when we came inside our houses.

"Tell me more about the Children of Melchizedek," Mrs. Carlisle said. "Did they ever speak of what they wanted to destroy?"

Eleanor didn't know. She said she had seen a map. Her father beat her for having looked upon it because he said the large paper spread upon the kitchen table late at night was a new form of scripture that would lead to the land of glory for the Children. It was pretty. There were lines all over it and I think those were highways. There were two blue snakes that met and became one snake, and her father and the other men had circled a darker area where dark lines were closer together like pieces of a quilt sewn together to make a patchwork. Momma made a patchwork quilt but she wrapped Sadie in it as she wept and we set Sadie in the Earth and my father screamed that his child's death was the work of man and I was frightened because I knew he would beat me if I even thought out the map and all its lines. But now that I have put it all behind me I want to know what the work of Man is. I want to imagine that those blue snakes are rivers and the dark patchwork is made of streets just like this one. I want to learn to read the names on the map so I can remember what it is my father and his brethren want to destroy to pull down the works of Man before the Lord Almighty.

Mrs. Carlisle asked Eleanor if she would like to take a train trip on her next day off and Eleanor was very happy replying that there had been cars and trucks and once when her family was still a family and they were driving along the highway and trying to ignore people in the other cars who stared at them because they mistook them for you-know-who down you-know-where I looked up and above me, there was a long silver train with windows moving faster than a bird chasing a fly on a summer morning, and I asked what it was and before my father could hush her words my mother said it was a train. Not just any train but a passenger train and it was heading to the city. It was full of people who were reading newspapers or books or just minding their own business and admiring the scenery as they rolled past it and they were calm. That's when my father pulled the car to the side of the road and beat my mother in a ditch. I cried but I told myself that someday I would be one of those people on a train.

So three days later Mrs. Carlisle woke me earlier than usual and made me garlic eggs and we got in her car and went where she said it was downtown, but not you-know-where down. The light was reflecting off the glass of tall buildings. The street was a rainbow I had seen once on the creek at the edge of our hog farm, and I hurried to keep up with Mrs. Carlisle who stood in line and bought two pieces of cardboard and called them tickets from a woman who sat behind glass. I heard voices like angels speaking to me from the air and then Mrs. Carlisle took my hand and led me to the top of a staircase with a number in lights on a sign at the top.

That's when I saw my father and his friends. They used to say only sinners ride on trains. They are sinners because they stare out their windows and look at all the poor folk and do nothing for them. How could they? They were travelling. Sinners have to go somewhere. That's why they ride the train.

He saw me. He saw me like he'd seen a vision and he stared at me. I wanted to call to him but Bob said I mustn't have anything to do with him again and I was frightened because I didn't want him to beat me anymore, not there, not then. And as we descended the steps I could see the train. It was silver and had dark windows that were staring with mystery and just as Mrs. Carlisle and I were about to grab hold of long metal handles and step up to the train my father grabbed me by the arm so tight it hurt and raised a hand to strike me but his palm never touched me because the hand of the Lord came down as if it was smoting a fly against a wall and the station exploded all around me. I said don't to him but he wouldn't listen so I pulled away and he called after me, but I ran as hard as I could to the far end of the train and Mrs. Carlisle leaned out from the top of the steps and called my name but my father shouted Thy Will Be Done and Mrs. Carlisle and my father disappeared and I got knocked to the ground as if it was the hand of the Lord and everything was smitten if that's the word for being smote and I tried to say don't but nothing would leave my lips except blood and blood is holy so I was certain the Lord was there among us because the train rained down on me in pieces of metal and I had to love the Lord because there was no other choice that I still wanted to say don't.

Crokinole

I looked forward to seeing Cody at the cottage every summer. We used to be good friends. Our grandfathers taught us to swim and dive off the dock. We learned to fish in the tea-coloured waters of the lake though we never caught anything. On rainy days when there was nowhere to go, we played Crokinole on the screened porch of our cottage.

The rain would form silver droplets on the wire mesh that kept the mosquitoes out. After hours of shooting for the pocket or bouncing each other's discs onto the floor the nails on our middle fingers would be black and blue. Then one day it all went wrong.

Near dinnertime, Cody and I were in a dead heat for the daily championship. His grandfather, who I partially blame, kept whispering in his ear. Mine sat back with his arms folded, a pipe between his teeth, and his chair tilted on its back legs. That's when I fired the fatal shot. I split Cody's favourite disc in half and leaped up with my arms raised.

My friend ran out the porch door. He was crying. The game must have meant a lot to him. His grandfather said, "See what you've done?" and trailed after his grandson.

That night my grandfather shook me from my sleep.

"Get up!" he shouted. "The cottage is on fire."

My family ran outside. Cody was illumined by the flames.

"Who's the loser now?" he said as he vanished into the pines.

Merganser

Mergansers look like loons but not really. Late on summer afternoons when the sun appears dusty from a long hot day in the sky and the jet skis have all been put away so the madmen who race the engines that sound like mosquitoes first thing in the morning, roaring up and down past the cottage, go out and eat their dinner at one of the few restaurants in the area and then drive home drunk and knock over deer and foxes on the highway, maybe a porcupine and a few skunks, a parade of mergansers floats past the dock. I pretend I'm asleep. I want to make them think I don't notice them. But I do.

A merganser is like a loon but it is a bit more interesting. It has a red crest because it saw a similar crest on a kingfisher and though he could look like that bird, though it just looks goofy on the lesser bird. A merganser doesn't make irritating, haunted sounds on foggy mornings when the water is still. It doesn't want to bother anyone. It just wants to look after its kids until they are old enough to have friends down the lake who are around the bend. It is the males who lead their merganserlings in a parade to the nest. Don't ask where the mother merganser is or the teenage daughter they hatched together. I don't know where the females are. My wife is friends with the local Avon lady and she helps her unpack her wares and my daughter has friends out there somewhere she says she can only get to in the runabout that came with the cottage rental. They disappear in what amounts to a Bermuda Triangle of invisibility so I pretend I am invisible, too, and pull my green-brimmed Coast Spotter's hat over my forehead, fold my arms in front of me as the merganser and the little merganserlings paddle past, and sit very still.

I identify with the merganser. He also has red hair although his looks as awkward on him as mine does or did on me before it went to find my life. My wife says I dwell on the future too much. The merganser also never lets on he is seen or being seen. I call that focus. Maybe self-discipline. Or maybe it's just because he's on vacation and doesn't want to be bothered by stuff. The parade of mergansers swings close to the dock because I know he is teaching his offspring how to be curious while remaining safe. Loons don't do that. They stay far away. They are cowards preened in their own image, a kind of fashion-conscious bird that poses for the camera in a society page, and they probably don't bring a cooler of beer down to the dock with them late on a summer afternoon. I think mergansers likely drink beer when they think no one is watching. They have that 'I'm still here but I'm chill with all this lake stuff' attitude that comes after the sixth or seventh empty goes back into the cooler.

This merganser guy is protective. Where's his wife? Does she want him to start the barbecue? He probably laid in steaks for dinner and they're sitting in the darkness of the cottage refrigerator and calling out for him – 'Moo, moo, I'm here and I'm waiting and I bet you are hungry.' But the merganser is responsible for his brood so he's not about to leave the cottage unlocked and go look for everyone. He never leaves a chick behind. Now and then he glances over his shoulder. He makes sure the kids are all there. He won't leave any of his brood behind.

My guess is that he works hard all year just for a handful of those days when, around five o'clock, everything stands still, including the kingfishers who, by rights, should be competing with the mergansers for the fish that stock the lake. But the kingfisher realizes the guy works hard and has mouths to feed, and I bet he flies to another lake – there are lakes everywhere – picks up some fish and leaves them where the mergansers will find them. That's kind of nice of the kingfisher. He didn't have to do that. The little mergansers turn to their father and say, 'Hey, look Dad! Fish! Let's have fish for dinner.' And he doesn't have to fry it. I think mergansers would be overjoyed to find a sushi restaurant, perhaps order a couple of plates of sashimi, and then drive home sober as a church mouse on the cottage country roads. No deer or foxes would be killed in the making of the day.

I say this because there comes a time in a merganser's life when he realizes loons are going to get all the credit for being lake birds and the merganser will have to raise his little flock with the awareness that the big-time action, the thrill of being seen and becoming icons of some social milieu that didn't invite him, won't happen for him or them. They have to settle for being mergansers. They won't dive out of sight like celebrities pursued by paparazzi and they won't grow up full of themselves. They won't be daunted by who they are – second place in the pecking order. Why should they? They do their own thing. Mergansers don't need others to notice them or tell them if they are important or not. Mergansers probably have a call, though I can't say I've heard the lonely call of a merganser and it summed up the illusion of a crowded vacation region as a place of solitude and spiritual mystery. There are no revelations or spiritual moments of insight associated with a merganser.

The merganser's world is what it is. There's water. They go for a swim. There's air. They'll learn how to fly. The merganser isn't told he has to reschedule his vacation weeks because the new guy on the sales team really, really, has to visit Bermuda because he's already paid for the flight and the beachfront hotel suite with a jacuzzi in the corner of the room for him and his girlfriend or some other place the merganser can't afford. He just says, 'Fine,' and throws himself on the mercy of the people who own his summer rental and, because he's a merganser and hasn't asked for anything before, this once, just this once, yes they can do him a favour although the two weeks will only be a week and a half because they have cousins coming from Cincinnati.

And after the parade passes there are dragonflies that circle and dart above the water. There are even more of them along the shoreline. Mosquitoes are everywhere. They are the hard part of a vacation. They don't like mergansers and they leave one itching all night because the drugstore in the nearest town fifteen miles away just sold the last tube, 'Sorry.' The dragonflies, some blue, some yellow, some a sort of silvery gold, are having a field day and eating their body weight in the little blood suckers every ten minutes. They look like the Battle of Britain. Good for them. Do you think the kingfisher will help them, perhaps pick off some of the slow-moving members of the evil little Luftwaffe squadron of useless blood-sucking insects? No. The kingfisher shrugs. He knows he should do something about the mosquitoes but he's waiting for a fish.

His royal red-crested, blue feathered whatever he calls the top of his head, is waiting for that one moment when a nice, big, juicy lake trout or maybe a salmon that found its way up the channel will come just that little bit too close to the surface and he'll pounce like a dive bomber and he'll leave a portion of his grand dinner near the merganser's nest because he knows his fellow bird has a lot of mouths to feed and because he's already king sitting up there on the hydro wire and he doesn't have anything to prove, unlike the merganser who knows he wants more out of life but realizes just raising his kids, just showing them the ins and outs of the shoreline and teaching them how to survive and be good birds is his calling even if his daughter and wife don't come home until its too late to barbecue and he's already eaten a bowl of Corn Flakes and called it a night.

Windmill

The long stretch of sand between the brown salt-stained cedar shingles of the well-to-do beachfront cottages began at the public beach and ended at Windmill Point. The footings of old piers that stooped to the waterline and the clipped wings of the windmill were all that remained of the old river-mouth industries. The last business to disappear had been sea-grass harvesting. Saltmarsh reeds were cut low every summer and bundles of grass were hung to dry golden before they were shipped overseas to thatch rooves or become horse fodder.

The old man used to tell me to look for what was missing if I wanted to understand what a place or a person had been.

"Absence," he said, "defines things."

He told me his wife had passed away but I didn't comprehend how grief becomes a way of life. He needed someone to hear his rambling stories. If we found a widow's purse in the high tide mark, he would bend down, cradle it in his hand, and shake the black skate fish eggs that rattled inside then tossed it aside.

One day he asked if I was thirsty and said his cottage was just beyond the dunes beyond the posher vacation homes. I nodded and followed him. I waited in the living room and said he would pour a ginger ale in a minute after he went to the washroom. A black handbag sat on the coffee table. I wanted to pick it up and shake it, but I dared not open it or rattle it for fear his grief would tumble out.

He emerged from his bedroom, clutching his bathrobe shut with one hand and holding a five-dollar bill in the other. He asked if I was a good boy who wanted to earn five dollars and he extended the note to me saying he would pay me if I did as he asked. The robe opened and he was naked.

I stood up and ran from the old man's cottage. I ran up the beach crying and terrified he might be chasing me. That night, as the rain pelted against the window of our rental I thought I saw him moving among the pines and could not close my eyes. I prayed my vacation would be over soon, and I stuck close to my father as he lay face down on a beach towel until he stood up and announced we needed one final swim before we packed up for the long drive home. The whole time my father and I bobbed in the waves, I was certain I could see the old man standing among dunes with his hand buried in his trousers.

As we drove along the Mass Pike toward the Hudson River, I imagined the old man standing at the edge of the town beach, and when my mother said we had crossed the Hudson I was finally able to shut my eyes. She asked me if I had enjoyed my vacation and said we'd return to Windmill Point next year because that's where we always went. It was tradition. I told her I wanted to go somewhere else and didn't want to go back there again.

The Loft

Crissy had two options: she could live in her grandmother's yellow clapboard house on a side street in the middle of town or purchase one of the new lofts converted from a Nineteenth-century cotton mill beside the river. Her Nanna's house needed a lot of work. New paint, a kitchen floor that had bowed beneath the weight of uncles who hovered around cooling baked goods, and an attic where bats got in.

The loft was fresh. Thick pine floorboards had been sanded and exuded the aroma of forests buried in the woodgrain restorers had sanded smooth. The beams were impressive. They had once supported massive looms. The space was open plan. It suited the lifestyle Crissy pictured. The rear of the space featured a view of the river that once drove cotton ginnies. If she opened the casements on a summer night she would be able to hear water passing over the cobbled stream.

Crissy told her friends her life was her life, not someone else's she inherited. The quaint furnishings of the old house were auctioned off. From the sale of her Nanna's home Crissy acquired the loft, new and comfortable leather armchairs with a matching sofa, copper pots she hung from a rack above the kitchen counter, and a comfortable bed. She settled herself in the loft and was certain she would be happy there.

For the first five nights in the loft, Crissy slept well. She couldn't recall having slept so deeply. But on the sixth night, she dreamed. She woke in the dark, her body drenched in sweat, ill to her stomach, and certain she could still hear the sounds of machinery from a dream. She stared across the dark space. She was certain she saw a child on the sofa, weeping and holding her hand, but the spectre vanished as she stared into the darkness.

What she thought she saw upset Crissy. As she sat and sipped her coffee in the morning, she wrapped her hands around the large mug and wanted to put the night behind her. But gradually she was overcome by a terrible feeling that the child wanted to speak to her. The longer Crissy stared at the sofa, the more the river sounded like machinery. Crissy needed a walk to clear her head.

The bright sunshine of a late September morning should have made her feel alive, but she couldn't get out of her head the image of the little girl. The longer she thought about the child, the more Crissy could see the details of the visitor. The girl was wearing a white pinafore over a dark blue gingham dress, black tights, and scuffed work boots. The child's hair was tied behind her or cut short, and she was clutching her right hand as she sobbed. She didn't look at Crissy. She was staring into her hand and her face conveyed a horror that frightened Crissy and made her question whether her Nanna's house might have been the better choice. Everyone in that house had lived happily and most had died happily when they were home.

The old woman was a study in courage. She had raised four sons in the small space, had lost her husband to appendicitis and her second-oldest, Roy, in a small town in Normandy. The bronze star her Nanna received was always on the woman's bureau beside her brush and comb. And when Roy's spirit stopped and looked into the room where Crissy was sleeping, she was certain her uncle's spirit looked at her and smiled. He had come home one last time to make sure all was well and that his mother and brothers were leading the lives he wished he could have lived.

The loft wasn't homey. Crissy paused in front of the library and decided to go in. She told the librarian that she wanted to know about the riverside mill. What had it been like there? Was it a place of sadness or simply a factory where the workers produced cotton cloth? The librarian's face grew serious. Without saying a word, she led Crissy through boxes of local archives and handed her one that contained the records of the mill.

There were images of women and children, each standing beside machines. They appeared gaunt. Their eyes were sunken and stared at her through the veil of time. One woman had her hands folded over her stomach and the photograph revealed she was missing fingers from her right hand. So were several of the children. The machines had been designed for operation by the nimble-fingered. Bobbins flew across beds of thread and if the flyer became jammed the operator had to reach into the loom and free the flying projectile before the shuttle slammed the threads in place. The process was a matter of timing. A second's delay could result in a mutilating injury.

That night, Crissy lay awake. She felt ill at the thought of what had taken place in her loft. There must have been terrible pain and suffering where she was making her comfortable life, living her dreams in a place where others had fought just to make a meagre living. She was embarrassed to be occupying their space.

She heard weeping and saw the child again, this time holding up her right hand. The ring, middle, and little fingers were missing. She was bleeding profusely. She stared at Crissy as if pleading for help but there was nothing Crissy could do. A gulf of time lay between them.

As dawn arrived, Crissy rose from her bed to make coffee, exhausted from having been awake all night and feeling too terrified to close her eyes. And as she ran the water to fill the maker, she turned and on the countertop, beneath her glowing copper pots, was a tiny little finger, withered and dried yet still retaining its fingernail and the colour of its young flesh.

Flying Cowboys

Bernie should not have been in the family photographs. After he'd spent five years out west working as a cowpoke on a ranch in Alberta, he signed up for the Canadian Expedition Force's third wave and was killed at Festubert. There is a rule somewhere, that the dead aren't permitted cameo appearances after their demise.

But, case in point, there he is cradling my mother in his arms. Even though she was no more than a year old in the 1930 snapshot, she always insists that she is the baby though she has no idea who the soldier is. They look happy. She is laughing at him in contagious baby laughter.

Bernie had gone over the top to rescue a wounded mate who'd gotten caught between the lines and had gotten caught on the wire where he was repeatedly shot. He must have suffered, but according to someone in the same outfit who told my Gran about her half-brother, Bernie kept calling out that nothing could stop him from getting on with his life.

Second case in point: there is a professional photograph of my mother and father making their way down the church aisle after they sealed the deal. They are beaming. Of course, they are going to be radiant at that moment. There is no reason for them to feel otherwise. They'd each found the love of their lives.

Sitting in a rear pew as my mother and father exit the church is Bernie. He has partially turned around and is grinning at the camera. The brass number III for the Third Toronto Regiment is visible on his buttoned-up khaki collar. His hair is combed and he isn't covered in mud. He looks spiffy enough to pass inspection.

Not that I don't wish him well, but Bernie should be dead. When I was backpacking across Europe after my third-year university, I made a pilgrimage to the war graves of the Canadians who fell at Festubert. I saw his stone. The white marble marker looked like a false tooth.

My mother squints as we look at her wedding album. She pulls a magnifying glass from the cushion under her bum and scrunches her nose.

"Who am I supposed to see," she asks.

"Him, I say," removing a capped pen from my shirt pocket and tapping the man in the uniform. "Who's that guy?"

"He must have been a friend of your grandfather's."

"But his uniform, that collar, those brass numbers, and the maple leaf shoulder patch are First World War. Him," I say emphatically.

I go to her bookshelf. There was an earlier album. It contains pictures of men with sideburns and handlebar moustaches. There is a picture of Bernie in my great-grandmother's garden. Bernie has his arm locked with his mother's. He is her only son. He is bending forward slightly and laughing. My great-grandmother stares directly into the camera as if no one is beside her.

"That's Bernie," my mother says. He was killed in the war."

"He couldn't have been killed in the war and then show up at your wedding. Your grandmother would have said something about it being bad luck to have a dead person at a wedding."

I wanted to tell my mother there are scores of photographs online of ghosts intermingling with the living. Sometimes all they are is a hand on a shoulder, a spare foot if a group is seated, or a faded face in the background of a group shot. They remind me of the hand that comes out of nowhere in Da Vinci's "The Last Supper" that saws at the throat of the figure seated next to Jesus.

Snow was falling as I walked along the street from my mother's condominium when I realized I, too, met Bernie. I was three years old and playing ball in our backyard on summer day. My ball rolled under a rose tree and when I bent down to pick it up it wasn't there.

"Looking for this, kid," the man in the greenish-brown uniform asked me. He handed me the ball.

I stared at him. "How did you do that?"

He smiled.

"Nothing is impossible, little guy. Some things stand in our way. People call them obstacles, but they are merely what one has to go around."

That didn't make much sense. An obstacle is what bars the way. I wondered if obstacles are merely doors no one has opened yet.

I took the ball from him.

"Wanna play?"

"Naw. Let me show you some real stuff. It's called magic, though don't ask me how I do it because hell if I know. Sorry. Heck if I know."

With that, he lifted off and flew around the garden, not like a frightened sparrow but more like a kite or a dancer who had become weightless. He did a summersault in the air and then set himself down softly on his feet.

"Say, kid, what do you want to be when you grow up?"

"I like cowboys," I said. I was a devotee of Roy Rogers and his horse Trigger.

"Wait here," the soldier said.

In an instant, he returned. The cowboys were not like the ones I'd seen on television. They were stubble-cheeked, dusty, and dirty as if they'd just finished a cattle drive. Some smelled of chewing tobacco and whisky. They didn't jingle-jangle-jingle in their spurs but shuffled with their legs spread wide because their limbs had grown into the shape of horsebacks.

An older cowboy, Trail Dust Dan, with a weather-beaten face stepped forward.

"I hear you are a dee-vo-tee of the open range. Nothing like the open range. The stars at night are big and bright, and not just in the heart of Texas. As far as the eye can see, heaven is there. You'd think Heaven is enormous but the stars ain't that far apart. You can jump from one to another. Yep. There ain't nothing like them stars."

"How did you get here," I asked.

"We flew," said the spokesman for the wranglers.

"I'd like to see that. I have never seen flying cowboys. I've seen horses jump but never flying cowboys."

"We'll do one better, won't we boys? Let's take the kid up for a spin."

The soldier nodded it was okay.

"We haven't dropped anyone since, I guess, Jesse James. Most people say he was shot by Robert Ford, but that ain't true. James spent too much time in the saloon one night and he insisted we take him up for a ride, but we dropped him on his head. Butterfingers McBride over there was responsible. Butterfingers got his name when he dropped his six-shooter at a showdown."

With that I was airborne. Everything below looked tiny. I had never seen my house from a height. I didn't know there was an angle to my backyard or the neighbour, Mrs Cudworth, sunbathed without her top on.

"Yee-haw," one of the wranglers shouted as he spun summersaults and dove and rose and did barrel rolls in the sky."

"This is amazing," I said. "I never thought cowboys could fly and I never thought I could ride bareback on one. How did you learn to do this?"

Trail Dust Dan reflected for a moment. "I just woke up or thought I woke up one morning and I was lighter than air. I'd been asleep beside a campfire and I thought I smelled coffee one of the boys had put to brew, but when I opened my eyes, the coffee was spilt all over the place and I had an enormous hoofprint on my chest. The bottom line is you can't trust cows. The leader, a big bull, was angry because I'd gelded him the day before. Bulls don't like to sing soprano. So the bull organized a stampede. That's when I became weightless. A heifer I loved, broke my heart quite literally. I think the bull put her up to it. You know what they mean when someone says, 'Oh, he's full of bull?' Well, the heifer was. She was kind of fickle."

I asked the soldier if anyone had been fickle to him.

"Yep, kid. Life. You gotta live it but you can't trust it. It is joy and pain all rolled into one. Say, you haven't been to Heaven have you?"

"No. Why," I asked.

"I'll get in trouble, maybe half rations for a good part of eternity for saying this, but you just gave the smart answer the angels want to hear at the gates. People get to Heaven because they realize life is fickle. They forgive. They can't forget. Forgetting is difficult but forgiving is easy because you're acknowledging the one you're forgiving is fickle, too. Lead a long life and I'll take you there."

We hopped from light to light in the sky, and Trail Dust Dan plucked a smallish star and pinned it on my chest.

"Now you're deputized. We've formed a posse to capture Bottomless Bart, a low-down who rustles cattle. He's called Bottomless because there are no depths he won't sink to."

With Bernie and Butterfingers as my wingmen, we zoomed through the cosmos until we caught sight of Bottomless Bart. Bernie went around behind a star to get the jump on Bart and Butterfingers attempted to distract him. Trail Dust and I went straight for the rustler, but he dodged at the last minute and pulled my sleeve as we passed. I fell through the darkness when, out of nowhere, I was grabbed by Butterfingers.

"I have to make at least one catch right," he said smiling at me. Meanwhile, Bernie and Trail Dust lassoed the bad guy and wrapped him up in knots, and carried him to the loneliest star they could find. They returned with Bart's wings, though I couldn't see them.

"Well kid," Bernie said as we reached my backyard and the flying cowboys waved goodbye, "that's how it's done. I gotta go with them, but I'll be seeing you someday, in some way, and probably when you least expect it."

This leads me to Case in Point number three.

In the old album, there is a photograph of a young woman. On the back, she has written "With all my love to my brave Bernie, eternally faithful, Margot." The picture is shaky, blurry, and likely taken by my great-grandmother. Bernie is standing with his arm around the girl's waist. They are kissing each other and her left hand is extended toward the camera to show off an engagement ring. That's where the album ends. The next black page is empty.

If I see Bernie again, I will ask him who Margot was, whether a letter from her made him go over the top and through the wire to rescue a fellow soldier. Could she have written him a Dear John while he was at the front? Many soldiers said such a letter from home was worse than taking a bullet. The bullet kills. The letter wounds, especially the heart, and the heart grieves for what it lost until it reasons against itself. Bernie would probably say Margot was fickle, that while he was away at the war, she met someone else and her love for that person was deeper than her love for Bernie. She and Bernie only believed they loved each other but couldn't say if they did. That's how love dies.

Bernie shows up at family functions and when I try to chase him down to talk to him, he turns, smiles, and vanishes. On a summer night a decade ago, I was lying on a dock and looking at the stars with my daughter. She pointed into the darkness and asked if cowboys could fly. I was certain she could see Bernie with the cowboys as they cart-wheeled, swooped, and hollered yee-haw as they leapt from star to star. I knew beyond any doubt she was soaring with them.

Family

She greeted me with a hug on the pier in New York City.

The last time I'd seen Clara I was a child of five and she was blond and about to marry Saul. My father and Clara had the same light in their smiling green eyes. They looked so much alike that anyone could tell she was his daughter.

When the Germans came to our village they gathered the men and shot them behind the blacksmith's shop. Women who ran out to find their husbands and sons were herded onto trucks. My mother knew I was hiding under our shed but she did not turn or wave goodbye. That would have given me away. I never saw her again.

After the war, the Red Cross claimed they'd located my sister but when I arrived the wrong Clara met me. The woman in New York was taller and had black hair. She had brown eyes. What did it matter? Out of fear, I accepted the stranger's kindness. I thought I remembered my sister's eyes like my father's but the details blurred over the years.

The American Clara gave me a good life. I was all she had. I wept when she breathed her last.

I never found my real sister. Too much time had passed. Strife chews up families but time swallows them. So what is a family? Can anyone say? My sister, Clara, if she survived as the other Clara had, probably lost the light in her green eyes.

Beautiful

Lucy, the older, was assumed to possess good sense and would keep her sister Susan in line. As the door closed, Susan told Lucy it was time they had fun. Lucy warned they had limits. They'd been ordered to stay put, watch television or play a board game. Their mother had to see the doctor.

'Why does Mother get to wear lipstick when we can't," the younger sister asked. "She has a whole table of it. And she has bottles of expensive perfume. I think it's time we found out what Mom sees in all of it."

Lucy shook her head but followed her sister upstairs. Their mother's dressing table was covered in a fine dusting of powder. Tubes of lipstick and atomizers of Chanel lined up like chess pieces ready to be played. For two hours, the girls took turns painting and puckering their lips. Then Lucy bumped Susan's arm and a red line appeared on her sister's face.

"Look! We can be clowns," Susan exclaimed.

By the time their mother arrived home, the girls had red noses and mouths made enormous with a shocking shade of cherry. Their faces were powdered white and their hair stood on end as if they wore zany wigs.

"Do we make you laugh," Susan asked as their mother stepped in the door. Instead, she grabbed Lucy and slapped her across the face, and wept.

Lucy recoiled. "What's wrong Momma?"

Through tears, she answered, "I'll never see you more beautiful."

The Hens

So when he died, few mourned his passing except the small boy who lived at the end of the dirt road where all the roads in the county ended.

Was there any justice in the universe when he looked down the barrel of the old shotgun, pulled the trigger, and watched the flash of lights flare through the invisible fissures between his face and the site at the end of the weapon as the weapon exploded, blinding him in his right eye? The hens had been his prized pullets. They were plump and squat but laid eggs in quantities larger than any birds he had kept in his life.

Each morning he would check on his brood, but that morning, with the interior of the coop splattered in blood, he saw his hopes for the prize money at the fair dashed. A second or third-place payout at the county fair would help matters just enough to pay Morgan what he owed for another month.

Morgan knew how close the old man was to the edge, and the moment of default had come and gone with the old guy unable to offer anything other than an apology. At night, the old guy would sit on his porch and listen to the sounds of the chickens clucking in their shed and think there could be no happiness on earth like the happiness he felt in his bones. The wind stirred through the green tendrils of the willow beside the creek.

The Make-Believe Days

If they were old that day she would take pleasure in reminding him what he was supposed to do or say. There was always something to talk about.

One Thursday morning –Thursdays were the day they were permitted to spend time together – she asked him over a cup of tea as she poured and scolded him for adding too many lumps to his cup if he remembered Henry. He needed some clues to get his memory going.

"Henry, who owned the boat. You remember him."

"Yes. Didn't he take us through all those enchanted islands," he asked. "I seem to recall fishing off the back of his boat, the Tony-Girl, and I caught a flock of flying fish."

"The Afterglow-Girl," she corrected.

"And didn't I wonder if we could bring the fish home and have them swim in our garden pond?"

"That would be difficult. Fish don't like trains," she said.

"I thought you said we were sailing through enchanted islands," he replied.

"We take the train home from the island."

"That would be awfully difficult," he said. "Should we hold our breath if we go underwater?"

"The train is on the mainland, silly. The boat sails around the islands but its port is on the mainland and we take a train from wherever it docks. Is that okay?"

"Yes," he said because the future wasn't her fault. "And someday, I know, we'll go there together. More tea please," he said and she poured an empty cup.

The Lego Man

Timothy was told he'd never known his father. He found that hard to believe. Sometimes he would dream of a man sitting beside him as he assembled cars and houses from plastic blocks that fit together. He was certain those dreams were memories.

Timothy decided to build his own father with Lego. He made the man tall, though multi-coloured, and gave him a face that resembled his own so people would say, "You have your father's eyes."

The Lego man sat in the corner of Timothy's room and didn't speak or move though he was a good listener. He could tell him anything. Each night, he wished his father would become as real as the other dads.

Nothing seemed to have changed the morning Timothy realized he was late for school. Without looking, he darted into the intersection and felt a hand push him to the far curb as a truck screeched to a halt in a hail of Legos.

Timothy turned and stared in fright. The Lego Man had followed him out the door. He had saved Timothy but was now scattered in thousands of pieces in the intersection. Fighting back his tears, Timothy picked up as many blocks as he could but even if he cradled them in his jacket he left many behind.

The floor of Timothy's room was covered in blocks and he stepped on them in his bare feet. The pain would not go away though he still had his father's eyes.

The Corn Maze

Cory, our youngest, always hung back so it was no surprise when we thought we'd lost him in the corn maze at Taggart's Fall Farm Fair. We'd gone to buy apples and choose our Halloween pumpkin. I found Cory at the entrance of the labyrinth. The jack-o-lantern on his head looked just like him – even the same teeth were missing.

"Where did you get that?" I asked. He didn't answer. Petey never said much.

He seemed 'off' when went trick-or-treating. Teenagers two houses ahead were smashing pumpkins on the road. I hollered at them and they ran. Cory's nails dug deep through my sweater and left tiny bruises.

The kids and I called it a night and went home to sort the candy. Cory sat in the front hall. I could tell by his shaking he was traumatized.

"What's wrong, bud?" I asked as I knelt beside him. He didn't answer. "How about we take your costume off?" It occurred to me he'd had it on since the fair. He pushed me away.

"Halloween's over. You can take it off. It's going to smell and go bad."

He wore it to school the next day. I got a frantic call from the principal. Bullies had split Cory's skull.

"I've called an ambulance," the principal said, "but I doubt there's anything they can do. There's nothing inside Cory's head. His candle has burned down to a lightless stub and he's lost the glow in his eyes."

Numbers

Their relationship wasn't supernal yet. That's what he got for falling in love with another mathematician but love was a combination lock and the only way in was:

1. Numbers. Prime numbers, integers. Numbers in long columns. Values inserted in an algebraic equation that could be numbers but could be

2. Heartbeats when she thought he was asleep in her arms but in reality, he was counting her heartbeats, determining the rhythm of the blood coursing through her body, calculating her systolic, the force of blood against her artery walls, and her diastolic pressure between heartbeats when her body was solving a problem about

3. The months they'd been together. Had he rushed into their relationship? Had she not followed him? Was he alone and billeted for a conference in an abandoned hotel?

4. The purpose of delivering a paper to people who didn't speak English and he grasped why someone wanted to demolish the place because the windows let in the noise from the street where Avenue A intersected with

5. Or at least a street with the number five in it that wasn't as busy as

6. Which were all the numbers he could remember when he tried to call her. She said his silence hurt but he replied that love was remembering all seven digits and waiting for the final one to come to mind, the elusive—

7. Sum of Heaven they needed to work out, the solution to all equations in the dawn = seven answers or 28.

Father Christmas

Men disappoint themselves. They are hard-wired to believe they can achieve impossibilities. Eventually, they reach a point when they realize they will never be professional athletes or leaders of the free world.

The world is a mess because men cannot arrive at a state of equilibrium within themselves the way women assure us they can.

So after I died this Christmas in the chimney while trying to persuade my five-year-old daughter who wasn't sure she wanted to believe in Father Christmas anymore that he was, indeed, real, I overheard my wife being consoled by her friend Debbie.

Debbie led a difficult life. Her husband was one of those types who come home drunk and punched out the walls. They ruin things for other men.

Debbie convinced my wife her faith in me hadn't been worth it. That hurt.

"Did he have desires, needs he couldn't control?" Debbie asked.

It was none of her business.

"Yes. He ate too much chocolate. That's why he got stuck between the damper and the shaft. He'd fit the year before. But you know, men are pigs, really, because he didn't realize how much weight he'd gained. We buried him in his Christmas suit. He was a good provider, but he couldn't control his impulses and gave in to his urges."

I tried to make a bell on the tree ring so they'd be startled, but it just wouldn't happen for me. Only after they were gone did I manage a faint tinkle.

Marta by Moonlight

When we were young and began living together, Marta used to sing a song her mother taught her.

"*We were sailing along, on moonlight bay…*"

She would pause and say someday she wanted us to own a sailboat so we could go out on a lake and glide through broken moonlight on the water.

Her dream almost came true. We moved to a town located on a small lake. I took shipwright lessons and learned some of the finer points of bending lumber and setting pegs. I told her I would begin building the boat in the garage when it warmed up outside, but she said I should undertake the project in our living room. "It is cold out there," she said.

I was puzzled that she'd have me build a boat in the house.

She grew thin. Words ran and avoided her sentences. Dreams tangled with threads of realities. The past wasn't the past anymore.

"It is a shame about our old boat. Whatever became of it?"

"We never built it," I told her.

"I love to watch you work," she said. "It makes me so happy."

Just before she closed her eyes forever, I painted our boat. On the stern of the white hull, I lettered its name, 'Marta-by-Moonlight.'

"Let's go sailing," she said.

The boat was too big to leave the house, but I cradled her in it until we reached a shore where we danced by the light of the moon.

The Butcher's Boy

My father was hunched low over the steering wheel so he could see the numbers above the doors of the shops in his old neighbourhood. He had me calling out the numerals if I could see them through the heavy rain.

Some of the shops were boarded up. Others were dark. Only the corner store had its lights on. A man leaned on his doorframe to watch the rain.

"Why is four-twenty-nine important?" I asked.

"It's where I had my apprenticeship. I served the customers and wrapped the cuts in sheets of pink paper, careful to shake the blood off. Shiny side to the meat. Dull side out. The chill made my hands feel dead. Everything had to be done up right with pink tape sealing the drugstore folds and the price in grease marker atop the packet."

"I don't see it," I said.

"I still do. It's where I met your mother. She came in for calf's liver. Her mother had anemia though at the time no one knew was leukemia. Meat aided blood. I only met your grandmother once."

"Was Mom beautiful back then," I asked.

"She's still beautiful," he said. "Looks like it's gone. It was here. Your mother is still beautiful to me. I hope you find someone like her someday. I wish you'd known her longer."

"I guess we lose things."

"No," he said. "They're like rain on a spring night. They're our lifeblood even when the past is dead."

The Sunflowers

They were taller than her father. She adored their yellow petals as they flagged in the breeze. Some faces had already begun to drop their seeds, but one had lost its kernels in the shape of a smile and she said that one was her favourite. Would her mother buy her a bouquet?

The bundle lay on the seat beside her. They were still vibrant but she asked her father to hurry because some of the flowers began to look sad and she shaded them from the sun with her jacket.

She had wanted to grow her own sunflowers. Her mother had a framed print of a famous painting of them in the breakfast nook. Their yellow matched the colour of the walls.

By the time her parents remembered to buy a packet of seeds, the growing was well-on and every other plant in the garden had a head start. Her sunflowers were small and her mother warned they might not bloom even if they were brought inside before the first frost and then sunflowers need room to grow and lots of sunlight.

She named each head as she arranged them in a vase.

The next morning as she stood in the middle of the kitchen she wept. Their heads were drooping. Had they died in the night? She had forgotten to add water to the vase.

"They died of thirst in the night," her mother said.

The child cradled a head and refused to let it fall.

Rain

She knows I have an inexplicable fear of rain. She can't understand where my phobia comes from and points out the discrepancy between what I'm afraid of and what I'm doing first thing every morning when I step into the shower. Rain bothers me.

My glasses fog up. Rain has nothing to do with mercy if it runs down the back of my neck, especially winter rain when I forget to wear a scarf. That kind of rain and cold reminds me of dying.

Last summer was our first together. A relative loaned us a cottage on a northern lake. On the second day, it began to pour. The forecast was for showers for the rest of the week. There wasn't anything to do except finish a book I wasn't enjoying.

One afternoon she asked if I wanted to get wet. I shook my head.

"Not in our clothes. Skinny dipping. There's no one around, and you'd be just as wet on a sunny day. I caved. We were in the lake and we made love, and the rain was soaking my hair. I felt redeemed.

I didn't want to dry off, at least not like I had when our house-keeper locked me outside on a January afternoon when I was ten in the middle of a thaw. When I came in she wouldn't let me get warm, not like the touch of my wife's skin that dried in the air as we ran back to the cottage.

Here We Are

Below them to the south, the plains of Tanzania spread green and slightly dusty brown where clusters of broad-armed trees reached up as they were praying to the peak, and to the north lay the lusher, denser verdancy of Kenya. They had forgotten their binoculars. They had wanted to count the coffee farms.

Marie said she could use a coffee right then. She had twisted her foot on the way up and sat down to take stock of her situation and see how the ankle adjusted.

"Just think," said Jacques, "we are on top of one of the world's great mountains. What's next? Denali? Aconcagua?"

"This is high enough," she said. "This is almost at the threshold of heaven. No more peaks for me."

"But here we are," he exclaimed. "We can tell the marriage therapist how we conquered this challenge together. Let's have a selfie."

"Your selfie or my selfie," Marie asked.

"C'mon, smile for it."

Only her mouth smiled. "We conquer places but cannot begin to overcome ourselves, and that's the sad part. Look at it all. Aren't we more than this? We've become tourists visiting ourselves. We talk of Arctic ice-floes or mountaintops. But what if we just sit on a beach or beside a lake and let it conquer us?"

"What are you saying?" His momentary triumph was becoming another moment of defeat.

"Well," he said, "let's enjoy it. Here we are!"

"It is all uphill with you. We're always trying to get somewhere but we never arrive at a place where we can say 'yes, we're here.'"

"We'll get there someday," he said in an attempt to put her at ease. The thin air wasn't good for her breathing or her heart.

"I probably won't arrive with you, and I don't know if I even want to catch up. Go on without me."

"It wouldn't be the same."

"Yes it would," she replied. "I'm just your shadow and you never turn to see if I am there no matter how long I've tried to follow. If you went without me, you wouldn't have a soul, and what is a person without a soul if they are standing on top of the world?"

Autumn Leaves

We got the call early on a rainy autumn morning. We were asked to come to the hospital as soon as possible. My father had taken a turn for the worse and though I questioned the nurse she would not provide more information. The leaves were wet and shiny, but most were trodden on the sidewalks by passersby. When we arrived, he was gone.

On the days he was away on business trips, especially rainy autumn days at the end of September, she played Roger Williams' recording of "Autumn Leaves" on the hi-fi turn-table and listened.

She was married on an autumn day, though not a rainy one. I found a red leaf she'd tucked in her bouquet and ironed between two sheets of wax paper nestled between the pages of a book she'd treasured since childhood. Her wishes had come true as the leaves could not hold on and boughs dropped a summer's work and the world died of another season. Dreams live forever but not dreamers.

My mother stood at the foot of his bed and told me her wish – that I would know the happiness that had defined her life. I wanted to tell her how time sets limits on experiences, that it tugs at the summer until its best work falls away leaving only a pile of bone and brittle branches, but it didn't matter what I said though the colour red has always reminded me of brevity in all its glorious grief.

The Sunfish

A Sunfish, little more than a large surfboard with a removable keel aft of the mast and a mahogany rudder at the stern was the best the old man could do on short notice. It was high season when the idea of being a pirate or a sailor for an afternoon filled his grandson's imagination. There were so many sailboats in the Sound with brightly coloured sails they jostled for ocean. The boy said "aye-aye to his grandfather even though the old man couldn't hear a word.

The reality was that his grandfather was not a sailor but a rower. Before the turn of the century, the old man's family owned a cottage on one of the islands in the Great Lakes. His elder brother came down with appendicitis one holiday weekend. Their father was busy working in the city. His brother didn't make it to the hospital in time.

Over breakfast, the old man said that tacking was going one place when they meant to be somewhere else, but that did not help them avoid the white, thirty-foot party launch that sounded its horn. Just before the collision, a man hollered through a megaphone their sunfish was in their path. It wasn't a flying day. The waters were calmed.

The old man pushed his grandson off the sunfish with his foot.

The boy was wearing an orange life vest and bobbed in the waves calling for his grandfather, and the sea tasted salty like his tears.

Philbrook's First Law

Everything has to happen in the correct order or nothing happens at all. That's Philbrook's First Law of Circumstance. I subscribe to it on metaphysical grounds.

This morning, I dropped the orange juice carton on the floor and my toes stuck together. I wanted to sit down and separate them with a damp dishcloth but my wife had tossed it in the laundry the night before.

I went to the laundry room and discovered our daughter's hamster had died in the night and because she'd already left for school I looked for a box, hamster-size, in which to lay Rudy's body in state on the kitchen table until my wife got home and we could discuss how to break the news to Polly. Polly adored the rodent.

Polly must have had a premonition of a death in the family because she was sent home after saying she felt ill. When she saw Rudy with his little legs in the air she sobbed that I had killed her pet.

I reassured her I hadn't. The pet shop insisted Rudy was female. Gus, the predecessor, showed no interest in his cellmate and the two fought for control of the wheel.

Their fighting was all for show because no creature wants to be denied the happiness it craves. I told Polly that's where babies come from, especially her, and that made her happy even though she was mourning Rudy.

"Why," she asked.

It's Philbrook, I said. "One thing just follows another."

Katherine Mansfield's Cello

Young women of wealth and privilege required a good reason to leave their homes and travel halfway around the world to London at a time the city was the center of Bohemian culture but when Katherine Mansfield, an heiress to one of the wealthiest families in New Zealand announced she intended to study the cello her mother did not object. Music was culture. Wasn't that a good thing?

The problem with the cello, as her mother discretely pointed out was that its ample body, pinched at the waist and cradled between her thighs presented the illusion that the player was in the process of making love to it, the way a lover might rest against a woman to catch his breath.

"But isn't the music divine," her daughter responded. The young woman had a point.

The piano works of Edward Elgar, in particular the "Salut D'Amour," had rehabilitated the instrument to some degree. Its pinched waist and long neck could be overlooked because the notes that emanated from the strings were doleful and resonant. and spoke of the difficulties of the human condition – the pain and the joy of suffering – that permitted one to glimpse a plateau far above reality and the grubby cares of working life. Unlike a human lover, a cello never complained, never sweated, never wanted more than what a player asked of it. The instrument was the ideal man and its notes vibrated through Katherine's lower torso and caused her to dream of the music that she assumed, was the melody of the soul.

Within a week of her arrival in London, a time too brief even to send a cable to her parents to tell them she had arrived in the heart of the world and the city was different from how she remembered it when she had visited it with her sisters during their grand tour five years before. She had been too young, perhaps, to appreciate the wonders that spread before her. 1908 and the five years since her previous visit had changed everything and she drank in the energy of the dirty air as if was an elixir.

She was standing in a music shop, picking up sheets of the latest songs and humming them to herself and wondering how they would sound if she played them on her cello when a young man walked up to her and invited her to join him at a tea shop several doors down The Strand.

He said his name was George. He was a painter and of all the young women he had laid eyes upon in London, she looked the part of a true artist.

"What does an artist look like," she asked.

George couldn't answer, but by early evening he was lying beside her in the bed of her studio and he said he finally had an answer.

"An artist is someone whose eyes suggest they are going to fail at life by refusing to fail in art."

"Isn't that rather morbid? Are you suggesting I am suffering from a malady of some kind?"

He replied, "No. You have yet to learn what you will give your life to accomplish." He was cradled between her thighs. His body was hot and heavy. His sweat stuck to her skin. She began to loathe her cello.

In the morning, much to her surprise, she found herself standing in the Registry Office of the Old Bailey and agreeing to spend her life with a man who might as well have been an understudy for her cello. What did she know about him? Love should always be the undiscovered country of the soul, and the more one knew of it the less one might feel the desire to explore it. She worried about how and when to break the news to her family in New Zealand.

She needn't have worried. The next night George did not return to her studio and she sat on the edge of her narrow cot and wept, not from a broken heart but from an absence of knowledge and her failure – not his – to comprehend what marriage meant when one was married. Certainly, matrimony wasn't about love, but neither should it have been about being abandoned.

On the third night, George returned. He could barely stand. When she asked him where he had been he beat her and walked out again.

That was married life. Love and marriage, as far as she could tell, were not connected the way a red rose might have grown around a briar in an old English folksong. There was no pea-green boat for her and George to sail away on. When she picked up the bow, turning the keys to tune the instrument that no longer spoke of the world. The sound was very wrong. The cello no longer wanted her.

Fourteen years passed. Her brother was killed in the war. So many young artists and writers and painters she had known were gone now. Her mother was dead. Her love affair with David was the beginning of the end for her. She had been living in poverty and contracted the wasting disease from him – the malady that fires the imagination and impels the soul but burns the body down to the stub of a candle until its light extinguishes itself.

She and a woman friend relocated to a pension near Fontainebleau in France.

The concierge and the gardener carried her to her room and laid her in a narrow bend and she wondered who owned her cello now – she had pawned it in desperation – and what they might be playing and if it loved them as much as it had loved her. As her eyes grew heavy with the setting sun through the tiny window that overlooked a railway yard, she wondered if she could write a story about her cello and whether it offered true love or merely a love song crying over the world.

Day of the Dead

Annie was aching to see Pedro. She needed him so very much. His absence felt like death and her empty arms were almost numb from the pain of missing him.

Pedro lived in Galeana on the other side of the grey saw-teeth of the Sierra Madres In the late afternoon light with the sun behind them, they traced the jagged outline of an enormous beast with a rough back. The nearer she approached, the greener the slopes became. She had been warned not to drive alone over the Sierras on her own.

"A woman alone in a car," the man at the rental agency had said in a whisper as he leaned over the counter.

The road snaked through the mountains. The shoulders were narrow and in some places non-existent, especially on the turns, and if she had to pull over for any reason – goats crossing the road, a flat tire, or simply to admire the green view on the steep valleys on the lush Caribbean side or the bone-coloured hills facing the interior once she went over the crest – she would be watched at every moment by cartel snipers.

"Why make a target of yourself?" the rental man asked.

Pedro had argued with her over the phone, the line cutting in and out. "Stay at an airport hotel. Don't make the journey alone. It is four hours from Monterrey. Why pay for a rental car? I can come and get you in the morning."

The thought of Pedro arriving in Galeana with an Englishwoman frightened her. The narrow streets, the shops where nothing much was sold because nothing much was purchased, the relatives crowded into a cinder-block room, and the whirr and clunk of the malfunctioning air conditioner, were things she did not want to encounter. Pedro had made it out of that world. He was a telecom engineer. He travelled the world and earned good money. They'd met in Zurich. Pedro, dark, suave, the epitome of Latin elegance and refined manners, and she, the clever Oxbridge technologist who knew all the answers except the ones she was working to find. They fell in love while having drinks and conversations about 5G. They both agreed they held the future in their hands.

But the more he attempted to convince her, the more assertive she felt she had to be. After all, he was not only in love with her. Love is a reciprocal arrangement. If she let him have his way with how she came to him, he would have his way with everything.

She'd been to Galeana once already on a brief trip. It seemed a dream to her. There was a village she wanted to see again. She had fallen in love with it as they walked hand-in-hand through the ancient streets.

Iturbide stood on the crest of the highway. It was shady and green, the last breath of the verdant before the descent began and the Joshua Palms with sea urchin spines stood amazed and abandoned to die in the desert.

And it was the day of the dead.

What better place to see the shrines and the Calaveras in the quiet square than Iturbide? People with faces painted as skulls, white, morbid, and surprised by death, would be kneeling in the square, offering shot glasses of reposado to their ancestors and reminding themselves of those whose features had faded from memory by placing sugar skulls on the cenotaphs. So many never returned to the mountain village.

She was almost certain she was entering Iturbide. As she slowed her rental and rolled down the windows, she could hear the bell tolling for vespers. An old woman in a blue skirt would be tugging at the lone bell rope that hung as if it were the snake from paradise creeping down the white stucco tower of the church. The front wall over the door would be red with bougainvillea and she imagined the Crown of Thorns, the suffering and blood that defined the Mexico she loved as the fluttering red petals. If the wind came up, they would scatter, pulsing from a sacrificial wound.

But she was not in Iturbide. Not the Iturbide she remembered. There has been a town hall at the far end of the square. A youth dance had taken place after school. Pedro explained it was a way to keep the young people in the sleepy town. They would grow up, and marry. They would live in one of the old, low, brightly coloured houses on the side street. She'd seen couples and their children, making their way up a side street and she understood how important love is when it is asked to bind people not only to one another but to a place.

Pedro and she sat on a park bench and talked about death.

"There is no death for us, at least not the way you see it, Annie. You've been taught to grieve for what is lost permanently. We have been taught to respect and worship those who are dead. Each year, the day after your Halloween, we have the Day of the Dead. We call upon the saints, but we also call upon those who walk with the saints in the twilight of a dusty autumn day. My grandmother, my father, my aunts, and my uncles, all live in that twilight. When you return, I hope you will return on the Day of the Dead, and I will introduce you to them all and you will hear them speak to you in the silence."

When she parked the car she was certain she was not in Iturbide. Had she taken a wrong turn? Highway 58 leads directly to Iturbide. There could be no mistaking it. All she had to do was follow the road toward the sky and then leave the sky behind. The church was not where she remembered it. The square had fewer trees. The bell rope ran inside the church rather than dangling free on the outside. She missed the bright red flowers.

A group of women with their backs turned to her, black shawls over their heads, and long dresses with elaborate embroidery were kneeling beside a shrine, laying kernels of coloured corn on the ground in the pattern of a multicoloured flower. As Annie approached, she thought it odd that the women were picking the sugar Calaveras from the shrine and eating them. From what she knew of the tradition, the candy sugar skulls were only for the dead. Another woman reached up and took a shot glass of tequila that stood beside a faded antique photograph of a man and downed the drink in one mouthful.

"Perdóneme. ¿Es esto Iturbide?"

One of the women, her face deathly pale as the bleached sands of the desert, her eyes blacked out, and her teeth painted on her lips and cheeks as if death had stripped away her flesh looked up at Anne and said nothing.

The bell was tolling. The women who kneeled at the shrine picked up their skirts and ran toward a procession as it left the church. Annie followed. The procession moved slowly.

The priest at the head of the line was swinging his senser. The smoke was sweet, almost sickly, but it held a bitter tang as if it were smoke that had been retrieved from the ceiling of a church after a mass and mixed with the scent of cigars and cooking and chocolate that had boiled over into the fire.

No one spoke. Everyone's head was bowed. The silence, the reverence of dusk when not a bird chirped or a rustle of a long dress could be heard, was mesmerizing. Annie wanted to embrace it. She felt as if it was a part of her that lay waiting in her soul that she had not yet discovered. And when the gate on the cemetery opened with a cry, Annie could see the arid plain below her, the graves packed as tightly as white bags of sugar, and each resting place was decorated in a photograph of the deceased and flowers, and seeds, the sugar Calaveras.

The priest, who was also in a Calavera face, raised his arms, and the women, the men, and the children moved toward the graves until they were standing on top of them. An elderly man and a woman embraced. A man put his arm around the boy and the boy, with blackened eyes, looked up at the man. A woman held a sleeping child in her arms. All had the white faces of the day painted over their flesh. And with that, they sank into the resting places and vanished as the sun sank over the village and the sky became dark.

Annie sank to her knees and began to pray for the dead. She wanted to whisper words of thanks but was overwhelmed and astonished by the silence. And when she opened her eyes, she was alone among the graves. The white paint had worn off the stones and the crosses. The monuments were toppled, and the walls were rubble. There was no priest, no flowers, no brightly coloured petals, no sugar skulls or shot glasses of tequila or small loaves of bread for the dead. Even the vista of the arid plain to Galeana was shrouded in fog.

As she made her way back to her car, the village, the church, and the side streets were in ruins. The square was empty. The shrine was gone. This was not Iturbide. Whatever this place was or had been left her feeling cold and empty inside. Had she taken a wrong turn?

She had no idea where she was.

Doubling back the way she came, as the darkness deepened, she kept checking her cell phone to see if she had any signal. She would call Pedro. She would describe the place where she had stopped. He could direct her or come for her.

She thought she heard his voice on the phone as she pulled off at a white roadside shrine in the valley. The shrine lay at the foot of an Aztec or Toltec rockface carving of a hunter. Pedro had told her it was an ancient prince who claimed the green valley as his private hunting preserve. The figure, known as Antares, had slid from the mountainside one day when an earthquake shook the valley. Nothing remained except the carving of a foot and a dog barking at the hooves of a deer.

"Pedro? Hello? Can you hear me?" He was breaking up. Only parts of words reached her. "I'm lost. I took a wrong turn. I lost something in myself and for a moment I was certain I found it. I found it in this village that vanished around me. Hello?"

The only words that came through were "San Sebastian" and "bridge."

She sat in the rental car and wept. San Sebastian? She scanned the map the man at the rental agency had given her as he warned her about travelling alone on Highway 58 from Linares to Galeana.

"That is a difficult route. You would be advised to go back to Monterrey and cross the Sierras there. The way south, even though it is less picturesque and through the desert, is the safest. The truckers use that route unless they are in a hurry."

There was no San Sebastian on the map.

When she was a teenager, Annie stayed up all night with an elderly aunt in the Midwest US who was addicted to Broadway musicals. A late show called Midnight Matinee on a channel almost out of reach of her aunt's television antenna was playing the almost forgotten Rogers and Hammerstein musical, Brigadoon, about a Scottish village that only appears once every two hundred years because it is cursed. The only thing that can break the curse is if someone, on the right day, stumbles across the town and falls in love with a certain woman. The townsfolk are destined to fade in and out of eternity. Annie tried to imagine what eternity would feel like – the cold, the endless darkness, the wind on an autumn night pulling the temperature down from the sun and casting it into the grave. The feeling of nothing except longing. The love that was always on the other side of the mountain and, as in a dream, the road that would not lead to that love no matter how many times a person travelled it.

San Sebastian. Annie pictured a martyr, tied to a tree, being shot with arrows. His suffering eyes. She had seen paintings of him in the National Gallery. The young man with curly hair has his eyes raised to heaven as if asking when his suffering will end, when would he walk among the dead and they would be among the living if only for a day, and where the bridge was between this world and the next.

Annie thought for a moment that Mexico contained the secret of what that bridge was. Moving from death to life and back again, crossing the vast void with every sense – sight, sound, taste, touch, and smell with the volume turned up as high as it could go and blaring the world into every thought – was not just a matter of standing on one's own grave and eating the sweet marzipan skulls that were only fit for the dead, but a desire to assert love even if it meant negating the self in white face paint, and flowers woven in black braids of hair and permitting death to enter the world so it can live forever. She closed her eyes and thought she was dreaming when she opened them, to the sight of children in bright paper costumes, their faces painted white, their teeth outlined in black upon their cheeks, and their eyes two sockets of darkness with eclipses in the centre of each. Each of them held out their hands as if asking for alms or inviting her to dance with them.

Scorcher

She has the volume louder than usual on the news radio station as they head past the exit for Canal Road. He begins to ask if she can smell the green onions ripening in the black soil of the fields but she shushes him to silence. She cocks an ear to the speaker in the car door to hear the traffic report. The road is shimmering in the heat as she slows to approach the line of traffic ahead where the car has come to a complete stop.

The sky over the city to the south is thickening with a tea-coloured stain as it always does late in the afternoon on a summer weekday. The air grows exhausted from overuse. He can tell even from the highway the labourers with their arms heavy and dangling must have been weeding since dawn because the backs of some with their shirts off are glistening in the sun.

"I don't like driving in heavy traffic," she says as she pulls out from behind a transport and speeds up in the passing lane. The road ahead is shimmering with the illusion of water. "This isn't fair," she adds. "Next time you have to leave suddenly just take a taxi to the airport like everyone else."

He knows it is not fair.

He thinks she knows the taxi would cost almost as much as the discount flight, but he has a plane to catch.

His best friend who lived several hundred miles away dropped dead while mowing his lawn in the heat the day before. Though they hadn't seen each other in twenty years, his buddy had been part of his life long ago.

The friend's wife had called from the hospital to say her husband didn't have many close to him from the old days, buddies from school

94

and university. In their time as roommates, he'd known her husband well enough to guess his wishes. She had no one to turn to. She asked if he remembered the night he'd introduced the two of them or the day he'd been their best man when the young couple ran down to City Hall between classes to be married. Their friendship has suffered from the pull of distance. They had grown apart, the miles between them and a disagreement making their friendship harder to repair after so many years, but she hoped he'd put all that in the rearview mirror.

When the weather and traffic reports are over and she turns down the volume on the radio, she asks what it was he was about to say. They were past that point.

"It was nothing," he says.

She shrugs as if she doesn't care and stares at the road ahead. A man with a tractor is plowing under a crop that has bleached blonde and brittle in the summer heat. He probably relied on the rain that hadn't fallen. As the tractor and its driver disappear behind a hill, he stares out the car window during the sports report his wife always turns down the sound of the radio and wonders how deeply the farmer feels the loss of his work or how the pain runs up and down the spines of the labourers. This shouldn't be a season of losses but they arrive and are beyond anyone's power to ignore. Heat sucks the life from summer.

"What did you want to know?" she asks again.

"I said it was nothing and now it's too far behind us to matter."

Bismarck

The arrival of a pack of greys was considered a key acquisition for our small civic zoo. One wolf would have sufficed, though it would have been a lone wolf in the truest sense. It would have bayed at the moon and howled as the other animals wrestled with sleep. A pack of seven howling together was unique. A closed-circuit video system enabled anyone to watch them online.

I pitied them.

Their enclosure might have been large enough to house a family of four living on a meagre income but it was far too small for a pack of wolves. The *Canis lupus*, dogs who haven't evolved into dogs, need space to track and out-maneuver their prey. A pack must hunt and put its natural sense of strategy to work if they're to eat. I've always been fascinated by the species. Dante was correct in *Inferno*. The worst sins are those of the wolf – the sins of premeditation and planning.

The Director of the zoo thought it might be offensive if children saw a rabbit trapped and torn apart which is how wolves eat in the wild. The pack was fed dead meat. Not long after their arrival, I stared through the observation window at them. I watched as they paced in circles. Their hackles never came down. Their pale, moon-like eyes did not look at visitors but stared into souls with an unnerving rage.

The arrival of the pack was foreshadowed by a media blitz. The newspaper held a contest to name each wolf. Names are important yet it is wrong to personify a wild animal. Each grey lived up to its name. The zoo presented the public with limited options. By the time someone was accorded a prize for naming each of the seven greys, the identity of each wolf was a *fait accompli*. A handful of people pick-eted the zoo entrance. They were upset the wolves had been given

German names: Bismarck, Guenther, Karl, Greta, Frieda, Mathilda, and Johann.

"I had no idea the wolf pack was going to be given names of U-boat captains and their wives," my neighbour quipped.

Those living near the zoo who often complained of the stench from the hippos or buffalos were angered by the howls of the pack when a full moon hung in the sky. Their enclosure was a prison without windows or doors. A blue light, supposedly a winter moon, lit their holding area. Their sky was nothing but artificial light, yet they possessed an uncanny sense of daylight and nighttime and knew, instinctively, where the moon was in the sky.

What the zoo did not take into account was that alone a wolf is no more intelligent than a dog, but in a pack, wolves are arguably the smartest animals among the fauna, problem solvers who strategize to find a solution to a problem. The keepers could not understand why, at night, the pack withdrew to the rear of their enclosure – a small concrete room where they supposedly slept out of sight where the lighting situation was constantly fluorescent and they had no shadows. A door had been installed so the handlers could enter the wolves' space if one became ill or to fix whatever was wrong with the exhibit.

No one noticed the old wolf, Bismarck, gnawing at the metal door handle and the surrounding steel of the room behind the exhibit area, and no one could have foreseen the breakout of the pack. Working as a group, they had gnawed their way into the drywall beside the lock. They must have heard the snib catch, the key turn in its tumblers, and the deadbolt slide into place. They finished their work by pulling the bolt receiver from the wall. With the lock out of the way, the pack worked the handle until it fell under the pressure of their fangs.

The next morning when the zookeepers opened the access tunnel to the enclosures – the penguins, the monkeys, the armadillos – they found the hallway strewn with the remains of two penguins and a small spider monkey. The wolves leapt out and the terrified staff barricaded themselves in a utility closet but not before one of them was so badly bitten that the doctors feared she would lose her left arm.

The escape of the wolves was the story I read after the fact. On my drive to work, I like to listen to music on the radio. The local station wasn't playing any of the top songs. Two reporters and a newsreader were exchanging updates and interviews with zoo officials. I thought it odd a zoologist was giving explanations of wolf behaviour so early in the morning. He kept repeating how he'd spent months in the Canadian forests, studying the habits of packs. I have heard wolves in the wild, too. Their howls are the sound of desolation and loneliness.

He described how the *Canis lupus* (he kept using the Latin name which reminded me of the suckling of Romulus and Remus by a she-wolf and how the word for a female of the species, *Lupa*, also meant prostitute) might behave in an urban environment. When he mentioned the animal's collective intelligence and the fact they talk to each other in a language we haven't deciphered I was at a four-way, waiting for the light to change. That's when the pack ran in front of me.

News is something that happens to someone else and at a distance, I'd always told myself. It isn't supposed to be personal but now it was right in front of me. A scratching tore at the back door where I have a spare car seat for driving my two-year-old to appointments and playdates. Someone or something was trying to open the rear door. The old wolf, Bismarck, appeared at my driver's side window. I was a mere inch from a wolf and he stared at me with his pale eyes. I felt as if I was alone and afraid on the shore of a lake in the Canadian Shield just as I had felt the night I heard the howling of a pack nearby. The light changed and I gunned it through the intersection.

Instead of heading to work, I pulled into an empty lot at an abandoned grocery store and called the radio station to give them the location of the pack. Wolves travel far very quickly. The intersection was at least five miles from the zoo. Although they had only been free for a few hours, they had been travelling fast and hunting squirrels in a local park. An elderly man out for a walk with his small dog was attacked. The man got away but not his pet.

I watched in awe as the pack surrounded a police cruiser on the street in front of me. The officer drew his revolver and fired a shot, and one of the wolves shrieked and curled toward its tail before writhing on the pavement and becoming motionless. A wolf pack's first principle is survival of the greatest number. Led by Bismarck who had caught up with me, they ran into a backyard and were surrounded by a high wooden fence. They were only a half block from an elementary school. I saw the patrolman follow them between the houses.

I pulled my car alongside his cruiser. He had a twelve-gauge from the seat beside him and was standing at the entrance to the yard. I approached him.

"Are you here to help or watch," he asked after a cursory glance over his shoulder. His name tag read Yolles. He was a young patrolman driving solo around the city. I had seen him once in a doughnut shop.

"We've got to stand our ground here. Are you ready to help?"

"I guess. I know how to use a gun."

He removed his side-arm and handed it to me by the barrel. "Don't raise it until you are ready to shoot. Make sure the safety is off if they come at you. We've got to keep them contained. The other units are at the lockdown to protect the kids."

I looked behind me. A woman and her toddler were standing on the front porch of their house to see what the commotion was about.

I shouted, "Go in and lock your door. The wolves have escaped."

She looked puzzled at first trying as she tried to comprehend what I was saying. Wolves? What wolves? There hadn't been wolves in this part of the country for at least a century.

My shouting had drawn attention to us. They came at Yolles who fired a blast that dropped a female. Bismarck was enraged and snarled, coming at us. I got off another shot that took down a male – Guenther, I was later told by the zoo's Director.

The pack recoiled.

I had no idea wolves could leap over an eight-foot fence, but in an instant, they were gone, disappearing in broad daylight into a wooded ravine away from the school. For the next eight hours, no one heard from the remaining four. They became ghosts among the trees. When I got back into my car I realized I still had Yolles' sidearm. I put the safety on and laid it on the floor of my passenger side.

When I went to the precinct to return the sidearm, I was asked to join a citizen's posse. An officer handed me a shotgun and I signed my name on some forms. I had never killed an animal before. Part of me felt I was defending my home and part of me was sickened by the act of violence. I wanted to go home, grab a cup of coffee, and compose myself. The desk sergeant asked me to stick around.

"We'll be needing you. You're to be deputized. We don't have the manpower to defend against these demons."

I wanted to correct him.

They were wild animals we'd captured and held against their will. They were only demons in fairy tales. Shouldn't the same rights we enjoy be extended to animals? Who was more vicious and strategic in their need to kill – wolves or human beings? After all, I told myself, humans are animals too although we rarely acknowledge it. I sat in the staff room and put my head down on the desk.

When I woke it was early evening. I stepped into the squad room. There were ten others there, all armed with rifles and shotguns. The remaining members of the pack were pinpointed in the dead-end of a ravine. We were to kill them. I heard the zoo Director doing a poor job of pleading for their lives. The police sergeant wouldn't listen. The hunt had turned into a deathmatch.

We were loaded into police vans and I was given a camouflage jacket to wear because I was still dressed for the office. We broke into two groups. I was on the slippery slope of the far side of the ravine. That's when we caught sight of the remaining members of the pack. Crouching upwind from the wolves, our commander motioned we should fire on his signal. I heard horrible shrieks, not just of pain but of fear as the creatures fell. The wolves had nowhere to run so they died in our trap.

Three of the pack fell with the first volley, except for Bismarck who, wounded, charged Yolles and bit him through the neck. I was on the left flank and the old wolf turned and ran at me. Then he stopped and stared at me. I looked down the barrel of the shotgun and pulled the trigger.

As the leader of the pack dropped, I could feel a part of me dying. Later that night, I wanted to stand in my yard, raise my voice, and howl at the moon behind the clouds. When the sky cleared for a moment, the moon reminded me of one of Bismarck's eyes.

Zebra Crossing

I have no son; I desire none.
Ben Jonson

Frank hadn't heard from his son today but he waited by the telephone thinking the young man would call and he could say hello and maybe talk about the old times. Even if his son wouldn't speak of it, there was a bond Frank felt with his boy. The last time they had spoken, there had been silence from his son's side of the conversation, but that was to be understood. A father knows there is always something that could have been done or said, perhaps a missed opportunity to grow close, that might have bridged the gap between father and son, though Frank could never say exactly what that bridge might have been. The mysteries of life haunted Frank, especially after Frank and his wife parted ways. Isolation is difficult terrain. There are never any obvious answers to questions of human connections.

They were both old enough now to live with the fact Frank and his son had gone their separate ways. His son would have a good job by now. The silences in their phone conversations suggested to Frank that his son was distracted by more important matters than speaking to his father. Maybe his son had a family of his own. Frank would ask but never got any answer. That kind of silence is excusable because it comes from responsibilities, and responsibilities become wedges between the generations. Frank could accept that. His own father had never said much to him no matter how he tried to reach out to his old man.

"You'd best attend to your boy," his Dad had told Frank one day when a phone call failed to make any progress toward them. Frank's father probably heard the sound of a child crying in the background.

The child needed something and was pleading. Frank was about to tell his Dad that the child was just a character on a television show playing in the background but the old man rang off before an explanation was forthcoming.

Despite their silences and the gaps, an unspoken love existed between father and son for Frank. He was proud of his boy. He had watched the academic parade across the campus from a college to the Convocation Hall but his son, even if he couldn't pick him out of the file of graduating students, was probably angry Frank hadn't applied soon enough for a ticket to the event. All the seats were gone. But Frank did snap a picture and he had a print made and would stare at it through a magnifying glass and think, "My boy's in there somewhere and I'm so proud of him."

Was it the canoe trip they took together after his son's second year at university where the trouble between them started? Frank could not remember what he had said or even if he had said it, but he thought he had given his son fatherly advice about being careful about the choice of mate the young man would make.

"There are some out there who you could fall in love with. They are beautiful and their beauty is mystifying, but in the end, they will break your heart."

He was trying to tell his son about a friend Frank had known for many years who fell in love with a woman because of her looks. After two decades of marriage, the friend had come home early from work one afternoon with a queasy stomach and found the wife in bed with another man. The friend took to the bottle. He let his health spiral until he suffered a heart attack.

"You need a good woman who will stand by you and who has your best interests at heart. A good heart is far more beautiful and long-lasting than a pretty face."

Had that been about the time his boy was dating a very beautiful young blond woman who wanted to become a doctor, and then wealthy, and then retire and go into real estate? What had become of her? Frank didn't have the heart to ask his son. The question would have invoked another silence, and the relationship between father and son didn't need any more of that if it could be avoided.

At high school, Frank's son had begun that phase of life as a star athlete. But the lad fell in with the wrong crowd. It was a story Frank had heard often from his colleagues at work at the sales office. They would look at Frank whenever he mentioned his son's problems, and say, "Sure. Kids are like that. There's no telling what they will get up to, isn't that right?"

Frank would nod. What could he say?

The older the kid got the less Frank felt he could reach him. Being a single parent was difficult. Frank was certain that if the boy's mother had been on hand she would have been the one to fathom her son's temperament and explain it to Frank.

He recalled that during their marriage, although those days were long ago and punctuated by a pain he did not want to revisit, his wife had been a natural psychologist. She read her son correctly. She could look at him, sit him down for a glass of milk and some cookies on a rainy afternoon when the boy came home from school, and in the hush of an autumn afternoon as rain pelted the window and the kitchen clock buzzed gently on the wall until one of them spoke, she would learn what the boy was thinking and feeling. The child revealed his thoughts to her whereas there had always been a reticence between Frank and his only child. Frank envied the mother-and-son relationship. Then, one day, his wife wasn't there.

His son was old enough to understand but not wise enough to embrace the meaning of death. His mother was gone. Each room of the house contained an emptiness in which Frank and the boy felt her absence – a cold, remote sensation as if she had never been there. The hardest part for the boy was going to school each day and watching as the mothers dropped their children off at the gate having kissed them goodbye and wished them a good day. Frank could never approach the gate or the mothers. He would take his son to the end of the street and then run to catch his bus to work, always conscious of being late.

There had been a moment, however, when his son was a little boy and Frank's wife was bedridden and dying when father and son were walking to a birthday party on a Saturday afternoon. Was it spring or autumn? Frank couldn't remember, but the rain was cold and his son was dressed in a yellow raincoat with a nor 'wester hat upon which droplets beaded on the brim before falling into the child's face. When they reached a major street, one on which buses ran and cars sped up and down the narrow lanes, they paused. His son pointed to the broad white lines painted horizontally in front of them on the roadway.

"What are the lines for?"

"The lines? Do you mean the white lines between the lanes of traffic?"

"No, Dad, the ones in front of us, the ones we walk over to get to the other side when the safety light flashes on the other side. What are those lines called?"

"That's a zebra crossing," he said, smiling at his son.

Through the rain on his face, the boy looked up at Frank and scrunched his nose. "Are there zebras here?"

"I don't think so," Frank said as he took the child's hand in his free arm while holding a shopping bag with the birthday present for the party in the other.

"But you say this is a zebra crossing."

"Well, that's what they call it because it has white stripes painted on the black roadway – like a zebra."

The child thought about it for a moment and when they reached the other side of the road he stopped, looked at Frank, and said, "I think there really are zebras here but you are just not telling me because you're afraid I might run out and look at them as they gallop down the sidewalk. What is it called when a thousand zebras run down a sidewalk and no one can stop them?"

"A stampede. And yes, stampedes are dangerous because if you get in the way you can be trampled and crushed."

"Do people die when they are run over by zebras? A boy in my class was run over by a car."

"Yes," said Frank. "That's why I take your hand. That's why I want to keep you safe. You're the only son I'll ever have." The boy nodded.

When they reached the front door of the house, Frank rang the buzzer. A woman invited them both to come in, but Frank said he had something else to do and he would return for his son when the party was over. The boy turned and smiled as the woman shut the door. Frank walked to the street corner and stood hatless in the rain with the drops beading on his glasses and the lenses steaming so he could barely see where he was.

He had forgotten what he had to do that afternoon but he remembered walking through the streets and seeing parents and their children ducking into shops and emerging with bags of fruit and butchers' parcels wrapped in pink paper. And when he reached the corner of his street he kept walking until he arrived at the hospital where his wife had died and where his son had been born.

An ambulance pulled into a circular driveway and attendants in long blue gowns helped the paramedics unload someone on a gurney that they wheeled into the Casualty Ward. In the distance, he could hear the whine of a siren weeping about the terrible things it had seen and complaining that other vehicles were standing in their paths and blocking the way ahead. "Seconds. Seconds. Seconds," Frank thought they were saying. Everything in the world was a matter of seconds.

He was certain he saw his wife or someone he thought was his wife boarding a bus, that slowed at a corner stop. When Frank had met her it was a rainy day exactly like that afternoon. He was soaked but when he looked up he smiled at her as he reached into his pocket to buy a ticket from the conductor. She was sitting opposite him and returned the smile, and his life as he remembered it had unfolded from that moment.

But the bus pulled away and Frank did not get on. He never met the woman who might have been his wife. There were no smiles exchanged, no talk of the weather or where her stop was. His future, as he thought he had remembered it, had never happened. He never met the woman on the bus, never courted her on a sunny summer afternoon in the park beside the canal. They never had a son together, and he could not say what had become of her or whether she lived on died. And the son he had always dreamed of having, the boy with whom he could reinvent the world, had never existed, though at the next corner as he stood waiting for the safety light to tell him it was safe to walk forward he had to wait as a thousand zebras stampeded on the other side and his amazement left him breathless.

Summer Placement

My uncle Henry knew someone who said something to someone else and that's how I got the job. It was hard work in the dark. The mosquitoes were usually bad. As we worked, Mike whispered, "No one wants to go quietly. That's the truth."

We'd follow Alf's car up a sideroad or a lane, turn off the engine and headlights, and wait. We weren't supposed to roll down the windows or let any air in because Alf warned us sound travels, especially music from a car radio in the dark, but that night Mike said, "Oh, to hell with it," rolled down the front windows, and the cool night breeze on our faces felt good.

Up the lane — it was nothing more than two parallel ruts cleared between the trees, I could hear someone crying. There was a thud followed by a long period of silence and Mike rolled up the window.

"You shouldn't have heard that, kid. You didn't hear nothing. Okay?"

I was good with that. Alf sauntered toward us. He had a baseball bat slung over his right shoulder so I assumed he batted left and for some reason could picture him standing in the box and staring down the pitcher.

"Hey kid," he said. "This is your co-op placement. You place them and co-operate with us and everything is good, okay?" I nodded.

"He works hard," Mike said. "He buries himself in his work." Then they laughed. "Karl says he'll hate to let him go at the end of the summer. He might have a future with us. Last year's kid talked too much, but this kid keeps to himself. He said he told his parents he was stocking shelves at a grocery store across town. His folks aren't the types to surprise him with a sandwich for his break. I think he's got a bright future. He's earned a college degree in something that has nothing to do with our business."

"Are you saying he's too smart for us?" Alf asked.

"No, just the opposite. I don't think he enjoys what he learned. He never talks about it."

"What did he learn?" Alf inquired.

"He knows how to write an essay and research stuff in databases."

"Sounds useful," Alf replied as he took a ghost swing in the air and Mike tucked into the dirt pile. "Do you think he doesn't approve of us? I mean, he never says anything and I'm wondering if he's bottling everything up inside him. It's a violent world and somebody's got to do it. Most of the stories anyone tells about it are violent in some way. It's like that Russian – what the hell was his name – who said everything is about love and death. I don't think the kid has been in love yet, at least not the kind of love that gives a person a profound understanding of death beyond just a summer co-op placement to finish his diploma."

"I think he's good at it," Mike said. "Look at him. The way he holds the shovel. The almost balletic motion of his torso as he transfers each shovelful. It's poetic, I tell you. The kid is focused. Focus is a big part of what we do, speaking professionally, and I would add artistically."

We dug in, shovelling the soil and patting it down, and I wondered who had been crying because I noticed in the purple glow of the moon when the clouds cleared the tracks of tears chasing each other down Alf's cheeks as we stepped out of the car and gradually the shallow trench the length of the man it held was smoothed over until the scar in the dirt appeared to have never been there. For good measure and because I felt a pang of grief for the man I had just buried because there wasn't time for any other formalities, I dug up a root of lane side flowers and planted them in the centre of the shallow grave.

Touch

When we were studying Anatomy in our program, Margot was my study partner. Later she was my partner on the job. We used to joke that instead of trying to describe the difference between the hippocampus and the hypothalamus we should study the ancient art of laying on of hands.

"Imagine how brief our work would be if we could cure by touch," she said.

I would point out that on weekends, our college, was devoted to animal education, and on a hippocampus, no rhinoceroses were allowed. The joke stuck. We referred to the college as "our zoo."

The early Christian Greeks called the practice of laying on of hands *cheirotonia*. The person doing the healing needed to be imbued with the Holy Spirit. That kind of divinity can't be taught, and no amount of laying on of hands could help someone in severe coronary distress. I would take our syringes of epinephrine over an Apostle any day. There are times when I wish we could engage the Almighty just a little more. He relies on us to be healers through science.

"Tell me a story," Margot said one day over coffee. "Lay one on me," I told her about the birth of my daughter. The baby came into the world with the cord wrapped around her neck. The child's head was aubergine. The tiny body was snow white. My wife wasn't permitted to hold her. The nurses on the scene put the child into an incubator.

A nurse handed me the key to the elevator and told me to run ahead to the neonatal intensive care unit on the fifth floor which for some odd reason was nowhere near the maternity ward. Once the team of nurses arrived, I was sent away. I wasn't supposed to see what was happening and if the child died I wasn't supposed to see it.

I had a coffee from a stand in the hospital lobby. After an hour I went back upstairs. All but one nurse had given up. The one who remained was doing Reiki on the baby – not touching her, but moving her hands over the infant's body to balance my daughter's energy fields. I dismissed the treatment as wishful thinking.

Things happen that can't be explained. During my wife's pregnancy, I sang "Somewhere Over the Rainbow" into her protruding belly and delivered a brief message to the baby.

"Hello. This is your Daddy speaking and I am looking forward to meeting you."

My wife questioned the purpose of the nightly ritual. At the time, I had no satisfactory answer. It was just something I wanted to do.

On the morning of my daughter's very awkward and dangerous entrance into the world, I decided to break all the protocols associated with a sick baby. When the nurse had her back turned, I went into the neonatal care area, pulled up a stool that resembled those old-fashioned spin-top seats, and opened the portholes of the plastic container.

The child was in distress. Her heart monitor looked like the Sierra Madres at sunset, jagged as shark's teeth and signalling cardiac failure. I put my hand in the box. The baby grasped my right pinky finger not because babies do that on instinct. That's when I sang to her.

By the time I had reached the midway point in the first verse, the child's eyes were open. She looked at me with astonishment as if to say, "I know that voice and I've heard that song." With that, her heart kicked into its correct rhythm. The monitor charted lines more beautiful than soft waves rolling ashore at low tide.

The nurse and a doctor came running because an alarm sounded on the heart monitor. Life arrived in the nick of time. I credit Harold Arlen with writing a good tune. My daughter claims it was a miracle and then holds her hands to her chin to make a frame and tosses her head from side to side as she smiles cherubically like a putti.

"Yes, dear," I tell my daughter. I let her have that moment and am proud and amazed she recognizes the frailty of her life.

Margot may not have been cut out for our line of work. One must be physically strong enough to transport a stretcher down a flight of stairs and back up again climbing and descending seven, eight, or sometimes nine floors. Going down is the hardest part. But more than possessing the required physical fortitude to do the job a person must have psychological strength. There are things we see that are difficult to talk about.

Margot dried her eyes. She reacted emotionally to things.

One warm, clear July afternoon, we were called out to the highway to help extricate a family from their van. The firemen were using a machine known as "the jaws of life," but the metal was too twisted to pry apart. A teenage boy was pleading for his life. The firefighters had removed the rear window, but the wreck was such a tangle the jaws would not work on the vicious puzzle that had been a family's vehicle.

The boy was bleeding out. We were running short of time. To extricate him, we had to amputate one of his legs. Through the haze of morphine we had given him, he kept saying he was a track star, an athlete, and he begged us to save his limbs. By the time we transported him to the hospital he was on his way out and he didn't last the twenty minutes needed to prepare an operating room for him.

That run hurt both me and Margot. We couldn't talk about it. We should have sought counselling but neither of us could spare the time. We could discuss mild coronaries of forty-something men who were back on their feet after a pair of aspirins. They were the ones who would walk away and wave to us after hours of waiting in the hospital.

Between the horrors, there were long stretches when we had to wait with our patients, and during such stand-by times, Margot and I grew bored with one another. There wasn't much we could say. I had a life, date nights with my wife, clever things my daughter said, and landmarks such as the day my child started school. Margot's life was her job. She never went out. Being a paramedic consumed every fibre of her being.

Late one night during a telephone conversation, Margot laid out her apprehensions as I tried to talk her into remaining on the squad. She was suffering from post-traumatic stress disorder. She always took other people's pain into herself. I don't do that. I look at what I do as helping people as best I can. If they recover, I figure they are alive because I was there when they needed someone, and fate and their health did the rest. Margot didn't think of the job that way.

"No one knows," she said, "and I want to keep it that way. I see people we've saved in the grocery store and I know I can't run up to them and tell them I was part of the tandem of paramedics who rescued them. I want to keep it that way."

I knew what she meant, but what she was saying was one of the first flags of burnout for people in our line of work.

Should I have referred her to our Employee Assistance Program? That would only add a mark to her spotless record of employment and unlike mine, I'd been caught eating a banana in our bus and I didn't have a chance to toss the peel away so it lay on the floor.

That's a no-no.

When my Supervisor wrote me up, I took the ambulance and drove through a car wash and a fast-food window because I couldn't stand the hospital cafeteria fare and I never bothered bringing my grub with me. The car wash was just for fun.

She never could romanticize a run to the hospital. I imagined we were the cavalry, the first responders on a scene who jumped in with our shirt sleeves rolled up to assess the situation and treat the patient. Margot compared wastes of time runs to firemen who rescue cats from trees. Her sentiments saddened me and I didn't know what to say.

Then came the February afternoon when we got a call along with the two reels in our firehouse. A pesticide plant had caught fire. There'd been an explosion and at least a dozen injuries. Green clouds wafted over the industrial east end. The police evacuated a nearby school.

The problem was not the fire or the injured who had made it out, but a group of workers in that far northern corner, the zero zone, who were still inside. Three walls and part of the roof had collapsed on them. They were trapped in the rubble and we had no idea to what extent they were injured or if some were still alive. The air wasn't breathable. Margot and I put on our gear – helmets, heavy boots, fire-proof coats and gloves, and respirators and followed the flame eaters into the mess.

We couldn't see in front of us. The FD went to work dousing the area with chemical retardants until a captain arrived from downtown and said the foam wasn't a good mix with the substances spilt inside the building. We were ordered to pull back. Our rig captain radioed we had to get out of there.

I obeyed the order but Margot refused and called me back.

"There could be people trapped under that debris," she said and began sorting through the collapsed building piece by piece. I thought of my daughter. I wanted to see her again but my training kicked in and I worked with Margot. She kept calling out in case someone heard her.

Our rig commander told us we had to get the hell out of there immediately. The danger of an explosion added to the chaos.

"We gotta go," I said.

"Go without me," was her reply. "Your wife and daughter want you home for dinner."

As I stumbled through the mess, I found a middle-aged man, barely alive, and put him over my shoulder to carry him to safety.

I turned and looked.

Margot had found a woman who was badly burned, coughing and fighting for every breath. My partner removed her respirator and put it on the woman who looked at her as if she had just met the angel of mercy. Perhaps she had. Margot cupped her hands around the woman's face and began mumbling a prayer. That was the last I saw of my partner. She was trying to heal the woman by touch.

I was about to go back for her when one of the crewmen on the rig grabbed me and held me back. An explosion knocked us to our feet. Three firefighters demanded the captain let them go back in. They were refused.

I was in a state of shock.

I hollered Margot's name through the ruins.

Then I had the oddest sensation. I felt as if a pair of hands were brushing soot from my cheeks and cupping my face.

I found Margot and the woman twelve feet from where I'd seen them last. Margot was still cradling the woman's head in one arm and attempting to protect her with the other. The flames had touched her, though not just in a lethal way but in a gesture of protection and giving of something so deep in Margot's soul I cannot name it, a comforting generosity of spirit so the patient wouldn't suffer anymore.

Resident

Dr. Coppard came into the surgical lounge still wearing his scrubs and a blue surgical cap. Frank's niece Marilyn and nephew Gary looked up, as the niece's son Tim remained buried in his hand-held video game.

"I am sorry, but your Uncle Frank didn't make it. The surgery went well, but his blood pressure and heart rate fell in the ICU and we couldn't bring him back. I am sorry for your loss."

Marilyn put her hand over her mouth, turned, and buried her head in Gary's shoulder as she wept. Dr. Coppard repeated, "I'm sorry for your loss," turned, and walked away.

"It has been a long day," Gary whispered as he tried to console his sister. "We're going to have to make all the arrangements in the morning, but it is late and we're both exhausted. I feel awful for Frank," he said as tears well up in his eyes.

Uncle Frank had been a fixture in their lives since their parents died in a car crash when the brother and sister were children. He was their only living relative, and though he had done it alone, he raised the pair, was always present in holiday and birthday pictures, paid for their educations, and was a grandfather to Tim.

As Gary drove Marilyn and Tim home, he wanted to say something – to ask if his sister remembered if Uncle Frank had any favourite hymns. Frank hadn't been a religious man. They'd never seen him pray. The idea of an afterlife, he once told them when they were out for Sunday dinner together as a family, was too much of a stretch for his imagination, and he added, "Why loiter?"

Gary swallowed hard and broke the silence. "He taught me how to tie a Woolly Bugger," he said.

Marilyn stared at the road ahead, and after a moment of silence, she burst out laughing. "God, Gary, the man loved to fish."

"It wasn't the fishing, though. It was the lures. He never cared if he caught anything as long as he tied his lures. All winter, he'd sit there at the kitchen table winding bird feathers around hooks and tying those tiny knots. I don't know how he managed to see what he was doing, but he always made those knots."

An hour had passed since the doctor came into the waiting room to break the news to Gary and Marilyn.

An orderly wheeled Frank into a basement room. It was cold. The cotton sheet they'd laid over him upstairs was flimsy. The blue hospital gown that was open at the back had been stripped from his body and tossed into a laundry hamper. Frank wondered why they had taken him to the basement. He felt slightly ashamed of his body as he walked down the corridor to the elevator. He should have taken better care of it, and he swore that he would, from now on, regardless of his age. The body is the house of the soul, he told himself. The basement was quiet. No one saw him as he reached into a trolley and pulled out a clean gown and a robe. They would suffice for the time being.

He went upstairs to the operating room where he had last been conscious. He'd made a mental note of the surgery's number, five seventy-five. Opening the door to the operating theatre, he saw Coppard working again, this time on a different patient. Coppard stepped away from the table and ordered his assisting surgeon to close. The assisting surgeon looked up at Coppard over his mask, and Coppard repeated, "I said close him up, now."

The woman on the table was wheeled up to Recovery, to the same spot where the orderlies had brought Frank earlier in the evening. He watched as a nurse stood over the woman and took her pulse. The nurse noted the details on the woman's chart that hung from a peg on the foot of the bed. The woman was barely breathing. She was not dead, but she was not alive, either.

Frank leaned over and spoke to her. "I saw what Coppard did. He left something inside you before he closed you up."

The woman opened her eyes. "Are you certain? I can feel something pressing against my lung. I was having stomach surgery, and its odd I felt something against my lung. Every time I breathe in, it is there."

Frank nodded. Before he woke, he had experienced a similar sensation in his left lung, the feeling that an ocean was flooding inside him, that something was pressing against every breath. "We need to do something," Frank said.

He bent over the woman and carefully peeled back the surgical tape that held her dressing in place. He felt her stomach and then moved his fingers to the left.

"I'm going to do something. He's left an instrument inside you. I'm going to untie the knots. Lie back, close your eyes, but don't go anywhere. Please don't go anywhere."

"Before I do," she asked, "where am I now?"

"You're in Recovery. Stay with me."

With the curtained drawn around the bed, Frank loosened the sutures. The surgical thread had been done up tight, but he recognized the knot and knew how it had been tied. He opened the wound just enough, to slip in two fingers and he pulled out a clamp Coppard had forgotten to remove. Then, Frank pulled the thread tight and re-tied the final knot. "I think that's got it," he said to the woman. "I think you'll be okay."

When the nurse returned to the cubicle in the recovery, she paused outside the curtain. The rule was that curtains were not to be drawn around a patient until they came out of the anesthetic. As the riders swept along the track, the woman opened her eyes.

The nurse asked, "What is your name and the woman replied, "Mary Stozle."

"How do you feel, Mary?"

"Much better now, I think."

"May I check your dressing?" asked the nurse. The dressing had slipped. "You must have pulled at your bandages. I'm going to get someone to examine the incision and make sure everything it okay."

"There was something pressing on my lung," Mary said, her voice raspy from the tubes that had been down her throat during the procedure, "but a nice man came and removed it."

The nurse went to get a resident and the wound was cleaned again and the stitches tightened.

"Leave your incision alone, okay?" said the young doctor. Mary nodded. The resident noted the matter on Mary Stozle's chart. "I don't get it," the young doctor said to her, "but just lie back and take it easy for a while. You're in good hands here."

Frank paused in the hallway outside the Recovery area. He held the clamp he'd taken from Mary in one hand, then paused, doubled over with a pain in his side, and looked at the floor as a small retractor fell from beneath his gown and sounded the note of a small bell. He bent down and picked it up. Coppard had left something inside him.

Dr. Coppard was considered the finest surgeon in the hospital. He had years of experience. Though he was seventy-five, the hospital board reviewed his work and his friends on the board had approved him every four months.

Mary was awake in bed in her room the next morning when Frank checked on her. After seeing she was alright, he went to the top floor of the hospital and followed Coppard from his office to the cafeteria.

He stood behind Coppard in the line as the surgeon selected toast, coffee, juice, and cereal for his tray. Frank wasn't hungry. When he reached the cashier, the woman noticed Frank had no tray. She appeared to wave at something as if telling him to move ahead through the line.

Frank was certain he had to be across town in an hour – Gary and Marilyn had an appointment and ought to be there – but he felt he had to say something to Coppard. After all, the guy had been sloppy and left something inside him; then, in the next surgery, had repeated the same mistake with Mary. He didn't want to be rude, but as Coppard sat down at a table, surrounded by his young residents who nodded to the older doctor deferentially, Frank set the clamp and retractor on the doctor's tray between the juice and the coffee.

"What the hell are these doing here?" Coppard shouted at the residents. "Is this some kind of a joke?" he demanded.

One of the residents looked up, and turning pale, said, "I don't know where those came from, but in your final two procedures last night, the chief nurse was short on her instrument count."

"And now they're on my breakfast tray? This is not funny."

"Dr. Coppard," one of the residents said, "Mrs. Stozle's incision had been tampered with. That clamp was the one missing from her surgery."

"You are out of line," shouted Coppard as he stood up, threw the instruments on the table, and walked away with his tray.

Frank stood outside the door of the hospital and tried to hail a cab, but none of the cabbies would stop for him. Other people got into the cars and drove away. Perhaps, he thought, they don't want to pick someone up who's only wearing a hospital gown. He went back inside to his room, but another man was lying in his bed, and the man was surrounded by strangers.

As Frank came to the nursing station, a woman in a hospital gown handed him a sponge, and as he tried to board an elevator, a young man with thin arms grabbed him by the shoulder and placed a broken scalpel in Frank's hand.

"I don't need these things," Frank said. "I just want to go home." The young man said nothing, turned and walked into a room. When Frank followed him, the room was empty.

Hours seemed to pass as Frank stood staring out the window of the lounge where Gary and Marilyn had waited. Every morning, when Coppard set his tray down in the cafeteria, sometimes seated among his esteemed colleagues or his student doctors, Frank would lay another small piece of surgical paraphernalia on the cafeteria tray between Coppard's juice and coffee until finally, one morning, the doctor did not appear in the cafeteria to eat breakfast with the others.

"Today will be the day I am fully recovered," Frank would tell himself each morning. "Today is the day Gary and Marilyn will bring me home."

Earth Hour

Her husband heard the birds singing and assumed it was time to begin the day. When he checked his watch, it was only two a.m. The songs were coming from his wife. She sounded like wild canaries and goldfinches.

The next day, the doctor listened to her lungs, and bronchia, and scoped her throat.

"Do you recall when the sounds started?"

"About a year ago. My husband and I were sitting in the dark for Earth Hour. It was the first warm night of the year. I stood on my front porch, closed my eyes, and inhaled deeply, so deeply I felt the world rushing into my body. The back of my throat was sweet as candied rose petals. The bird inside me I wouldn't stop singing."

"You've swallowed springtime," the doctor said. "It happens sometimes."

"Is there anything I can do for it," she asked. "Will the euphoria last? What's the name of my malady?"

"You have *acute avian dyspnea*. From now on it will return. If there's a blizzard remember to stand on your porch and exhale. You can't keep it bottled up after March. You'll see why."

At the end of summer, the songs ceased. She missed the birds until April.

She felt a lump in her throat and thought she might have cancer. Instead, she had a choking fit. Her face went aubergine as a small yellow warbler made its way up her windpipe, landed in her nested palm, and sang its heart out.

Constant

Every Sunday morning before the sun came up, our father would rouse the four of us from our warm beds and set us to work around the house. We could have understood getting up that early on that day if we had been members of a sect. Our call to action would have been measured in fervour or at least perceived that way, but we didn't believe in church things, as our father put to the neighbours. We, or at least he, believed in being busy.

If we didn't roll out of bed, if we didn't put our feet on the cold floor and line up to use the bathroom, we were lazy good for nothing. We were little bastards. That hurt. Our mother had been very loyal to him. Our job, our mission, was to clean the house from top to bottom. Mom had always kept the place spic and span, but after she passed – I was the youngest and was ten at the time – there was no stopping our father from taking up the cause of cleanliness. He would rant that his wife had been the patron saint of sparkling. The bathroom and kitchen faucets had to shine. Not a footprint could be seen on the living room carpet. My sister would vacuum her way out backwards. We learned a kind of sanitation engineering, how to do things in such a way as to magnify work. If we gave a window an extra polish with a soft cloth it would shine and reflect his face. If we worked the duster into the crevices of a picture or an end table, we could make the object appear new. My two older brothers couldn't hide the nicks and scratches on the furniture with the sweat and grease that beaded on their faces. We did everything to please our father. But there was no pleasing him.

After every offensive of hard labour, he would run his fingers over every surface of the house and claim that we had been sloppy.

By noon, we were exhausted. One day my older brother Roy walked out. He said he couldn't take it anymore. He told our father to get help. Our father replied that he couldn't afford a cleaner on one salary, that it was up to us to step into the void because our poor mother, the poor martyred saint, had worked her fingers to the bone and died for our sloppiness. She had been hit by a driver in the parking lot of our local mall while shopping for a Mother's Day gift for our grandmother.

None of that mattered. One by one, my older siblings fled. My sister was the last to go. She held up her hands one Sunday afternoon. Her cuticles were bleeding from the cleanser, the bleach having eaten away the natural lustre of her nails. She slapped our father's face and left an imprint of her blood on his cheeks.

When I was sixteen, I got a job working for a shipping company down by the lakeshore. The area used to have trucks lined up at loading docks. Emptying or loading a transport was a night's work, and the pay was good. I was saving up because I knew that I had to get away, and if I got away I was going to go someplace where I could get an education and become something other than an experienced janitor. My oldest brother had. Then he got into drugs. The rest of his short life was a mess. When they found his body in an alley, all my father could say was that he had died in filth. I wanted something clean.

The Sunday of my departure came when I was so bone-weary I couldn't move my arms. The night before, with a push on to empty three trucks rather than the usual one and turn around a shipment in record time – I imagined a man from the Guinness Book standing behind the plastic drape on the loading dock with a stopwatch and a clipboard, – though I wasn't sure who was keeping the records and if such records mattered.

He came to me at four a.m. His wake-up calls were coming earlier and earlier because he had stopped sleeping. I hadn't gotten in until three. When I heard his voice I told him to fuck off. He disappeared and came back with a bucket of kitchen compost and dumped it on my bed. "Look at the rot you live in," he yelled.

I got up, showered, shaved, then packed my bags. I had some friends from work who told me that if I ever needed to I could crash on their rec room couch. I did. I slept on that couch until I finished my final high school term. My father would appear on Saturday nights and yell at us on the loading dock until the foreman got tired of him coming up and interrupting the rhythm of our work and had him arrested. He had stepped on company property and that was trespassing.

My sister moved back to the city. Her venture out west didn't work out. The guy she had hooked up with, she said, was just as crazy as our father. She had done okay on her return, got a nice apartment, bought a car, and cleaned up her act, as she put it wryly. One summer evening we drove by the old house. It was for sale. We stopped and asked one of the neighbours what had happened to our father.

"You didn't hear? He spent all his time cleaning. We saw him scrubbing the driveway. He was down on his hands and his knees. We pretended not to notice because if people want to do weird shit, well, they have a right, and who are we to question. But we should have questioned. The hazmat people had to evacuate half the block. Your Dad decided he was going to concoct the perfect toilet bowl cleaner. He'd said something like that to Harry next door, and Harry told him to be careful. Your old man almost killed us. He'd left the window open and green clouds of mustard gas poured out and rolled down the street. A couple of boys were playing road hockey and had to be hospitalized. The old guy had mixed bleach and toilet bowl cleaner in a bucket because he thought the rust stains in the bowl were germs. He'd made about five, maybe six gallons of the stuff before it got to him. He'd set the buckets in each room. Maybe he thought he was going to let the gas clean the walls. Who knows? By the time we found him, he had drowned in his lungs."

My sister and I wanted to cry on the way back to her place. We had a right to cry. We couldn't. Our father had been the one constant in our lives, and he was gone. But after a long silence, as we turned onto the lakeshore expressway to head back to the comfortable mess my sister lived in and in which I was welcomed, I had to make a bad joke about it. She looked at me in shock for a moment, and then we both began to cry. The salt tears tried to cleanse our eyes but they only stung us deeper so neither of us could see where we'd ended up.

"We need to make a clean break from the past," she said, and realizing her words cut both ways, she pulled into an empty parking lot and shut off the car. We looked at each other through tears that couldn't cleanse our eyes.

Pas de Deux

I had a feeling Mossy would rise above herself and achieve greatness but had no idea her path to acclaim would begin the day we accidentally left her at the rest stop. In fairness to our parents, they had overbred.

There were eight of us jammed into a Town and Country, the kind of station wagon with faux wood panels on the doors and a seat in the back that flipped down into a three-seat space when we weren't picking up groceries. We never had enough money for loads of groceries, so I never remember the seat being down. I do remember Mossy sitting beside me and singing to a wilted dandelion she picked off the grassy median between the pumps and the highway.

By the time I noticed Mossy was missing, we'd covered at least a hundred miles. I didn't have the heart to tell Dad that one of us got left behind. He'd been a Marine and although the phrase was coined by the Navy Seals, he appropriated it for his own purposes: no one gets left behind. Instead of telling everyone about Mossy's absence, I took her dandelion and pressed it between the pages of a book about Dreadnoughts I'd found in the neighbour's garbage. I wanted to go to sea someday in a mighty battleship, but by the time I grew up, battleships were history. Five days, in fact, passed before our Mom asked what Mossy was up to. We all shrugged. Our Mom was cool about Mossy's absence. She didn't panic. She just continued making dinner though Mossy usually helped with the Shake N Bake.

Over dinner, Dad said they ought to do something. What if Mossy had been abducted by pedophiles, although he didn't use that word in front of us? He used the word "strangers." Then he went back to eating. Nine mouths saves money. Mossy would have been one mouth more. I often lay awake at night and worried about Mossy, but I kept having the strange feeling she was okay, that she was still alive, and people, maybe a kind couple, were raising her as their own and giving her the love and attention she would never have found in our brood.

My suspicions were correct. A kind couple did find her. They lived in the city. They had connections to a ballet school. What I considered to be underfed and malnourished, the ballet school decided were the perfect proportions for a budding prima. And though I wouldn't know Mossy's true story until years later when she appeared in the *Time* magazine I was reading while waiting for dental work – the bad mouth was a gift from my early years – I felt as if Mossy was narrating my thoughts about her. I could hear her voice. I would open my relic of childhood, the book about huge grey battlewagons, and stare at the brown withered stem and the curled, slightly yellow flower Mossy had left behind.

"Dear Bernard," she would always begin, as if my thoughts about her were letters I was receiving and she was the pen pal I always wanted but never wrote to, "I am having a wonderful time. The Gellers who found me at the gas station after you and the family drove away have been very kind. They have showered me with attention, gifts, and the education in the arts I always dreamed of having when I stared for hours at the flowers I'd pick. The petals of those flowers reminded me of tutus, and I knew I never wanted to return to my old life the first time I heard Tchaikovsky's *The Nutcracker* where, in the final act, the flowers come out and dance and leap in the air. I read later that the Waltz of the Flowers in a local radio broadcast interrupted the countdown of the test site for the Manhattan Project. The first mushroom cloud bloomed to the sound of flora leaping across the stage. I am fine. Think of me again, soon, your sister, Mossy."

A few nights later when I thought of her again, beginning my thoughts with "Dear Mossy, I'm sorry we screwed up but I am glad you are well," I found I didn't have anything to say to her. What could I say? Yep, we drove away. Yep, I noticed you were gone but I didn't want to get in trouble, so I simply let Dad keep driving. Yep, I bet you were petrified. Petrified is too weak a word. Crazed with horrible pangs of abandonment? And I imagine Mrs. Geller, she of the kind face and perfect couture mauve silk summer Chanel suit like something Jacquie Kennedy might have worn, walking up to you, bending over and saying 'Don't cry, little girl. Tell me what is wrong.'

The way I see it Mrs. Geller is as much to blame as me or Mom and Dad or our six siblings. The woman could have done something. She could have alerted the Highway Patrol or the State Police, and an all-points-bulletin would have blared from trooper radios up and down the eastern seaboard, and if they figured out where we were if you'd done as you were told and memorized the town our farm was near, then maybe justice, the big J justice, would have been served, but the small J justice of a little girl's life would have simply tottered along until you befell a fate worse than death, the fate of dying of unrealized potential. But Mrs. Geller had one thing going for her everyone else didn't: she wanted you. I stopped the letter in my mind. I couldn't sign it. I pictured the piece of paper and crumpled it up and tossed it in my imaginary waste paper basket.

Mossy must have known I was thinking about her because her voice appeared in my head like those disembodied voices that introduce old movies but abruptly disappear. "Dear Bernard: You shouldn't waste a lot of time thinking about me. I'm fine. I don't expend a lot of time or energy thinking about you or the other kids – Flo, Gare, Zane, Gimpsie, Cranleigh, or Melton. I hope you won't take this the wrong way, but they mean absolutely nothing to me now. I am now officially Mossinda Geller, the junior female dancer of the Eastern City Ballet. I danced the part of Marie, though in some productions I am her doll, Clara, and in other productions, I am the eleven-year-old girl Clara. Clara Stahlbaum. I am conveniently eleven, very slender, very light on my feet. Madam Karznikova has advised me to stay off pointe. Every now and then she picks up my leg, usually my right, draws her finger along the calf muscles and says 'You have all the makings of a prima, my dear. Build those legs. Stay off pointe. *Pliés* to your heart's content. *Tendu* so you feel like a willow in the wind. The more *Rond du Jambe* the better. But stay off pointe until you are seventeen. Most people suggest pointe far earlier but those dancers end their careers far earlier. Does any of this matter to you? Am I boring you? Such things may not be, nor may never be, part of your world. Best for now, your sister, Mossy."

I imagined being glad Mossy was getting good advice. I had no idea what she was talking about, but by then, Dad never got out of his chair. Mom stayed up in the bedroom all day and smoked, which eventually burned the house down taking with it Gimpsie and Melton. Cranleigh ran away from home. 'One less mouth to feed,' Dad muttered as he burned the Shake N Bake. I was old enough to walk to town and get a library card, so without anyone noticing after I had discretely checked out the book, I would slip a volume on ballet under my shirt and read it in the barn. No one went into the barn except Flo who had a home business on the side on Friday nights and weekends. If Flo found my book she never let on. She had other things to do.

When no one was looking, I would practice the various poses, the bends, the stretches. I learned the art and the benefits of standing up straight, and I figured that even if I amounted to nothing else I could always get work as a posture coach. One night as I was trying to write to Mossy in my head, I got the strangest idea that I should walk into town, withdraw all I had secretly saved in my meager bank account, and hop the next bus to the city. I mean, why not? I wasn't going anywhere standing still.

When I arrived, I tore a leaf out of the Yellow Pages in the bus station. I'd seen that late one night in an old movie and figured everyone tore a page from a telephone directory. A woman saw me and yelled that I was vandalizing public property. I wasn't vandalizing it. I was putting the information printed on the page to good use. The page contained a list of dance academies. There was one, Gerald Graham's School of Dance that was only a few blocks away. His sign had dropped the Gerald portion to make passersby think the academy had something to do with Marth Graham for whom Aaron Copland composed "Appalachian Spring."

"Dear Mossy: This will probably never reach you, but I have a secret to tell you. I used to stay up all night and listen to a classical music station through the static of the old Bakelite radio Gramps used to use in the kitchen, and I learned a helluva lot about symphonies and dance suites and chamber music, quintets, and quartets. I didn't dare let Gare hear me. He'd gone kind of rough. He beat up a kid at school for reading poetry. When I was about fourteen I concluded that Gare was going to rob a bank or kill someone someday and as the overachiever in the family, he did both. By the time I left home, he had left home, and I didn't expect to see him again.

Mr. Graham agreed to interview me for his academy. He moved about the parquet floor like a tissue caught in a windstorm. He was okay. 'Yes,' he said, 'you have raw talent but it is very raw and I see something in you beyond what I see in the raw,' so with that, he gave me a room atop the building, a broom of my very own, and told me that after I cleaned I should dance with the broom. Brooms aren't bad as partners, but they tend to stay in one place.

After five months of constant practice and continual cleaning, the Graham Academy presented its annual recital. Most of the dancers were little kids. The company was lacking in mature bodies, especially men, though Mr. Graham often auditioned lithe males he met on his nightly strolls through the city when he said it was good to get out and walk and clear the cobwebs from his head after a long day. So, Mossy, I have some news for you.

"Dear Mossy: It's been a long time. I haven't forgotten you. You wouldn't know me now. I quit the farm. There wasn't any future there, and not a lot of past. Our brothers and sisters, when left to their own devices, didn't cope very well with their imaginations. You could say most of them hit brick walls. I left. I'm in the city now. You inspired me to learn more about dance, even though in reality we haven't shared a word since the day we drove away at the gas station. I still have your flower. I have the *Time* magazine clipping beside it, the book I pressed it in, and the book on ballet that I took out on loan from the town library and promise to return someday though I suspect the overdue fine will be enormous. I am learning to dance. We had our recital. I was spinning in a *tarantella*, which you're probably aware is a kind of whirling Dervish dance of death. As I left the stage there was a Miss Parry who came up to me. One minute I was wiping my face on a dirty towel and the next minute there she was, shaking my hand, and she asked me to join her troupe. The troupe, though I'm not sure you know it, is the East Side Étage. I rehearsed with them for six weeks when Miss Parry told me that Bernie Crank wasn't a suitable name for a ballet dancer. I replied without thinking that all my family were Cranks, and she threw back her head and laughed and I laughed when I realized that, yes, my name was funny. 'Why not try Bernard Loiseau?' which means Bernie Bird, which is almost as bad as Bernie Crank, but saying something in French makes it more dramatic. Saying anything in French adds an air of class to the thing. So, that is how my career as a male principal began. You don't need to write back, but you should know that I have seen you dance as close as can be. You are exquisite. You didn't even know it was me.

Just before Christmas – do you recall the day your male principal fell and broke his ankle and then the understudy threw up from the flu? All those kids were waiting in the audience, children who belonged to parents who loved them enough to pay a hundred dollars or more a seat to let them see *The Nutcracker*. I happened to be walking along the street across from the theatre after Miss Parry took me to dinner at a very nice bistro.

Your Madam Karznikova came running out of your theatre. I could see the panic on her face. She recognized Miss Parry and looked me up and down and the next thing I knew I was waiting stage left for you to enter from stage right so we could dance the opening *pas de deux*, the "Dance of the Sugar Plum Fairies." I was Prince Coqueluche and you were the Sugar Plum Fairy.

Fate has a strange way of blinding us to everything except our training and our instincts in those moments when we pour our hearts into what we love to do. And there you were, on pointe, making your way to me, and I gathered you by your waist and after the entrée, the adagio, the variations, and the climax, I raised you high above my shoulders, turning round and round as if you were the sun, and your tutu reminded me of a dandelion blossom, its petals smiling at the evening light, as the world passed by oblivious to what it left behind.

Puzzle Pieces

Finding the letters bundled and tossed into the batting of the attic was a surprise. My wife and I spread them on the kitchen table. We knew her grandfather, Michael, had served in the Italian campaign and then in Holland. The stacks of correspondence and photos would have been museum pieces under any other circumstances, but the correspondence was not meant to be found. Who was Arthur? We were intruders into a dead woman's privacy.

A puzzle piece, like a letter, never tells the whole story. Too much was missing.

We could guess her grandmother had been in love with Arthur but after he shipped out she married a high school hero named Michael. Did she have a premonition of Arthur's death? What happened after the war? The passion Arthur described in his letters would not have ceased.

Both men survived the war. Had one been killed would the relationship have been simpler in a winner-take-all scenario? Michael had been an Air Force mechanic. Arthur was a foot soldier. Michael had been wounded when his airfield was attacked. Arthur led a charmed though arduous existence in the infantry. Both men had been afraid, but only Arthur had reached out to her grandmother with expressions of physical affection. Michael was staid and proper.

Love, even open honest love, is a puzzle at the best of times but those who solve it assemble the pieces until they form a picture with so many missing there weren't enough to say more.

The Ticket

When he was seven years old and the family farm was reverting to dust from fencepost to fencepost, his mother took him to the train station with a ticket pinned to his jacket and handed him a small suitcase.

"Never forget where you are from," she said.

After he'd grown up, gone to college, and studied constitutional law, the great aunt who had met him at the end of the line prayed he'd become a lawyer. He'd been in the army and would have taken up a career in the service until a three-year posting in Alaska broke his spirit.

When he was about to be wed, his wife-to-be asked where he was from. He had a hard time remembering. His aunt had never spoken of the place, having left the farm herself long before the life drained from it.

"Field," he said, though he told his fiancé he couldn't be certain.

"A name or a space," she asked.

He didn't know.

The summer after his wife died, he went in search of himself. He drove west. There were fields everywhere. If he asked had there been a Field nearby people would laugh and tell him to take his pick.

As the sun was setting, he pulled his car to the shoulder of an arid road and leaned on a fence post. He stared into the setting sun. It had a ticket pinned to its glow. The light had to come from somewhere if it ever wanted to arrive.

Eucharist

The dormer window of his room overlooked the low, rolling hills of Bordeaux, and on late summer mornings, after the stillness of the night and its stars had passed, a low mist hung on the tiled roof of the stone church of St. Perdue in the palm of the valley.

The room had been the domain of his grandmother's youngest brother who was killed near Verdun. The old woman refused to let his uncle's dress uniform be removed. It draped over a woven wicker seat chair and the officer's boots at attention with the toes facing into the room. Somedays his uncle would wear it again.

When the next war concluded, his mind was a jumble. He'd watched his boyhood friend being shot. His grandmother died. His dead uncle consoled him.

The village doctor suggested he plant a vineyard.

"Patience will soothe your mind."

His uncle, who became more alive each day, could work beside him.

His first harvest was not exceptional. A press they found in the barn was rusty. The vintage had a sad metallic aftertaste to it. He sat with his uncle and his boyhood friend in the dining room as they shared a loaf of bread. The seventeen on his uncle's collar glistened.

"It is time for you to leave here," his uncle said. "There's nothing for you to do. You need your studies."

"I know you'll work the vineyard," he replied. "Remember. Every sip, no matter where I go, will be in memory of you."

Conservation

When October rain worked its way between the layers of fallen leaves, her scent reminded me of the forest after we had walked all morning through the conservation area. Sunlight illumined small, glowing embers that were merely fallen leaves just enough to make me believe we were walking through a purging fire. She remarked others did not love us the way we love each other.

"Should they," I asked. "You're right. Our relationship isn't about them. It is about us."

"It isn't that," she said. "We deserve love because we give love. I'm talking about more than a reciprocal arrangement. I am talking about investment or time, feelings, and patience."

Her father had been an abusive alcoholic who took out his anger on the world on her mother. She had grown up afraid and had said she never wanted to be afraid again as she made me promise to be kind to her.

He turned to her. "Neruda, the poet, said. 'Let us forget, with generosity, those who do not love us.' I think about that often. That doesn't mean we are entitled to love. Entitlement is a rough road where giving becomes a form of demanding. I gather Neruda was saying something to the effect that we have a right to refuse to love those who hurt us. Even the harmful, the monsters, deserve some measure of dignity but we have an obligation to offer them absolution and mercy and never withhold the power that resides in our generosity of spirit."

"You're talking very altruistically," she said. "It is difficult to feel any of the spirit when someone is around the house ready to hit you without notice, or gut punch you if they come in late, reeking of booze, and so disoriented they had trouble standing up to put their key in the front door."

"We live as humble subjects in the kingdom of love. I live in the grasp of your love for me, though it is not about possession. It is about giving oneself to one's other, not as an object but as a subject in a very medieval kind of way. Look at those trees around us. Their arms are holding up the sky, but they don't own the sky any more than we can say we own the air or the sun or the breath we draw. We serve. We take, we give back, knowing that we are subjects not only to the world we share but to each other. Thine is the kingdom. You are the kingdom. I want this moment to live forever – you and me to live forever not just as flesh and blood but as boundless beings who are part of everything. That's conservation in its purest form."

She turned and looked away. She wasn't certain if I was mocking her or attempting to be empathetic and failing at it as I usually do, or simply blathering on as I usually do. There is a fine line between what I want to say and what gets said and it so easily becomes blurred. All the way home, and the next day and the weeks after that she said little and an icy silence settled in the space between us like a first white painting of frost on the leaves and grass, until one morning she woke and the entire world was hushed.

The snow was falling, muffling the sound of cars in our street. Even the paperboy beneath the purple sky of the first light and later the children passing on their way to school and walking entranced toward the sound of the school bell were hushed. The wind was solemn and hushed, and she said she had nothing left to give. I asked why she was going. She replied that everything has a season. Spring would come one day and maybe she would return like the Greek goddess who was called away to the Shades on days when there was nothing to hear and even less desire to say what might be heard. She added she would die without her new man, and my heart broke. I wanted to cry but she wouldn't hear my tears or see the words fighting to escape from my lips,

Neruda says there are emeralds in the earth. Crimson leaves are rubies. Removing them bleeds the earth dry.

"You'll get over me," she said. "I know you will try hard. I will try hard. Everything worth keeping is a touchstone against which each moment is tested and measured."

After she had packed her things and driven away, I stared out the window but what I couldn't see was what I couldn't hear and the longer I thought about what I had said during our walk through the valley as the trees shed pieces of their lives, the less I could remember our conversation. Memory becomes the silence of snow. The snow was falling now. Once the leaves are gone nothing can restore them to the barren boughs. All that remained was the voice of a prayer waiting to be said.

About the Author

Bruce Meyer is the author of 77 books of poetry, flash fiction, short stories, non-fiction, and pedagogical texts. His most recent books are *Grace of Falling Stars*, *One Sweet Moment*, and *Church Grammar*, and the short story collections *Magnetic Dogs*, *The Hours*, *Toast Soldiers*, and *Sweet Things* (from Mosaic Press). Winner of numerous national and international awards, and author of national bestselling books including *The Golden Thread: A Reader's Journey Through the Great Books and Portraits of Canadian Writers*, Meyer was the inaugural Poet Laureate of the City of Barrie. He lives in Barrie, Ontario, with his wife, Kerry Johnston, and is a professor of Communications at Georgian College in Barrie. In 2022, he received a liver transplant and continues to recover from it. He urges everyone to sign their donor cards.

Acknowledgments

The author is grateful to Trasie Sands of the South Shore Review, Halli Villegas and David Bigham, Crystal Mackenzie and the staff of Freefall Magazine for their support of "Pas de Deux" in the Alberta Magazine Publishers' Association Award, Nina Muntean and Lynn Hutchison Lee for their support as they prepared the *Through the Portal* anthology, Michael Mirolla who was my co-editor for *This Will Only Take a Minute: Canadian Flash Fiction* (Guernica Editions), Steve Carr of Sweetycat Press, Bruce Hunter, Marty Gervais, Antonia Facciponte, Amanda Quibell, and Dr. Carleen Lawther for their encouragement of my work. This book would not have been possible without the care shown to me by Nicoletta Cauccia, Salma Adam, Dr. Les Lilly, and the Transplant Team at UNH in Toronto. A very special thank you to Rahim Piracha and Howard Aster of Mosaic Press for their support and for believing in my work. This book would not have been possible without the love, care, and courage of my mother, Margaret Meyer, my sister, Dr. Carolyn Meyer, and my daughter, Katie Meyer.

And to my wife and guardian angel, Kerry Johnston, who has seen me through so many trials and tribulations and who has steadfastly stood by me with superhuman strength and determination to restore my health and voice.